BED
STUY

Praise for *Bed Stuy*

"In *Bed Stuy*, Jerry McGill crafts a love story that is as gritty as a New York sidewalk and as tender as a first embrace. Two people from different worlds grapple with the challenge of how to bridge their divides—made chasms by race, age, and privilege—to connect, to understand, and to forgive. McGill's knowing gaze is unflinching but compassionate, conveying in all its complexity the terror of love, the fear and doubt that plague it, and the bone-deep need for more."

—W. S. Winslow, author of *The Northern Reach*

Praise for *Dear Marcus: A Letter to the Man Who Shot Me*

"An unforgettable and intriguing journey . . . Violence, hope, despair, forgiveness, anger, and living with a disability are explored both lightly and deeply, humorously and profoundly, and always honestly."

—*Library Journal* (starred review)

"An inspirational memoir by a writer who refuses to be defined by his paralysis as he comes to terms with the unknown man who shot him."

—*Kirkus Reviews*

"I couldn't put it down. This is a compelling marriage of remembrance and forgiveness, absolution and compassion, cynicism and understanding."

—Wes Moore, author of *The Other Wes Moore*

"Written with passion, honesty, humor, and a stubborn, rebellious optimism, *Dear Marcus* is like nothing I've ever read. When a bullet in the back told Jerry McGill not to go on, Jerry went on—smiling."

—Shalom Auslander, author of *Hope: A Tragedy*

BED STUY

A love story

JERRY McGILL

Little
a

Text copyright © 2021 by Jerry McGill

Published by Little A, New York

www.apub.com

Amazon, the Amazon logo, and Little A are trademarks of Amazon.com, Inc., or its affiliates.

ISBN-13: 9781542030298 (hardcover)
ISBN-10: 1542030293 (hardcover)
ISBN-13: 9781542030304 (paperback)
ISBN-10: 1542030307 (paperback)

Cover design by Adil Dara

Printed in the United States of America

First edition

For Doreen, the most underappreciated person I know.
Thank you for passing on your strength.

It is a peculiar sensation, this double-consciousness, this sense of always looking at one's self through the eyes of others . . . One feels his two-ness,—an American, a Negro; two souls, two thoughts, two unreconciled strivings; two warring ideals in one dark body.

—W. E. B. Du Bois

An old black ram is tupping your white ewe.
Arise, arise!

—Iago

One

Of course, flame played a role. Flame had so much to do with his life. He remembered vividly how his mother would leave him and his brother alone all night, just children, while she hit the clubs with her girlfriends. He and Darnell had grown up fiercely independent. But on one particular February night, he fucked up bad. As had often happened in their Bedford Stuyvesant apartment complex, the lights went out. They called it a "power failure." It seemed like power had been failing him all his life. In this case, it meant no more television for him and his brother. But they needed to see. So he lit candles, six, maybe eight of them. Placed them in the kitchen and in their bedroom. Eventually they both fell asleep.

The smoke was the most devastating aspect. But he witnessed the violence of the heat: bright and infuriating. It was like a lizard's tongue lashing everything around it with a searing intensity that reminded him just how small and weak he was. Humans didn't stand a chance against nature. Never did.

The flame never reached his skin. But it touched Darnell. It touched Darnell the way acid rain touched a paper plate. The left side of Darnell's skinny body would never be the same again.

When the threat was over, the fireman asked the boys, "Why were you alone tonight?" Darnell, in fresh bandages, knew to clam up in the presence of white authority. Darnell didn't make the smart choices in life, but, unlike Rashid, he shared his mother's street smarts. It was Rashid who foolishly uttered, "She leaves us alone a lot." When his mother finally got home, euphoric off a night of dance and weed, the authorities confronted her with allegations of abandonment. The claim never went anywhere, but a certain damage had been done. A trust between the youngest son and his formidable mother had been eroded. Darnell became the one she expected to do the right thing. Flame taught Rashid a lot about the way things can collapse in the world, and that smoke, like disappointment, can spread rapidly, sticking to the walls forever.

But now, so many years later, flame was revealing something beautiful to him. For as he lit his cigarette in the cold windy alley behind Comforti's, she came out to join him. She had even brought her own cigarette; it looked a lot fancier than his—slim and pristine. Two years later, he would shake his head on the subway platform when he heard that song of theirs, and he would feel one small regret. *I should have just walked away.* But in that first shared moment, as he lit her cigarette, hand steady like a deer in headlights, he watched Rachel Pollack, took in her features, noticed there was a confidence about the way she stood in her flesh. Her skin was illuminated like the blood of peaches, and he thought that this must be a rare instance where flame could bring two people together. She had to cup her hands around his to keep the lighter from going out. The flame dabbed at her fingertips, playfully. Her hands were softer than those of the other white women he knew. "Sorry about my mother," she said.

"It's cool. I'm used to it."

"That doesn't make it okay. She is getting worse with age. I'm sorry."

"Really. It's fine."

"No, it's not fine. Your job is hard enough. Dealing with rudeness from the people you serve shouldn't be a part of it."

"It's okay, ma'am. Your mom is a regular. She's good people. She always tips well."

"You're a good guy. I bet your girlfriend appreciates you."

Words have power. Rachel Pollack didn't teach him that, but she reminded him of it more often than anyone. The first time they made love was two weeks after he first sat for her mother. Rachel took him to a Bronx hotel room after an afternoon spent at Coney Island. Their bed was right near a window, and moonlight mixed with streetlight caused the sweat on both their bodies to flicker like fireflies in a tunnel. She had said to him in no uncertain terms while digging her nails deeper into his shoulder blades: "Harder! Harder! I'm not a flower!" When he obeyed, he was rewarded. Later that night, over a lukewarm pinot noir, she would tell him his eyes reminded her of a sunset she had once seen in Salzburg. He couldn't picture what she was referring to. He hadn't left New York since he was a child.

He had no idea that sculpting was a job someone could make a living at, that a person could actually be paid hundreds of thousands of dollars for doing this thing that to a child in the classroom seemed like a messy bit of fun. In fourth grade he had shoved a wet mound of clay down the back of Tara Madison's blouse and been sent to the principal's office for it. His mother would later give him a beating for it (not the full belt; for that type of transgression, he got an open palm), but at least he had let Tara know he liked her. It established a pattern he'd revisit many times with many different Taras—attraction usually led to pain. But his personal impression of clay was simplistic: it was dirty and could lead to trouble. Gazing upon the professional pieces in Muriel Auslander's studio—he would later learn from Rachel that one had sold for six figures—he was mesmerized.

This woman is for real, he thought.

Rachel walked him to the far end of the studio where he stared in awe at the sculpture of a large and powerful Black man, a boxer, full figured, staring straight at him, a gray warrior frozen in clay.

"She met him at a gym in Detroit. He was training for the Olympic trials. He had a horrible problem with heroin, though. Died of an overdose in '96. His youngest son found his body in the bathtub, curled up in a fetal position. You ever try heroin?"

The question took Rashid by surprise. Heroin, like any drug stronger than weed, wasn't something he messed with. The question seemed inappropriate, out of place.

"I've never done anything heavier than weed. And I hate needles. You?"

He watched her face grow soft and then tighten, and it took her several breaths to respond. In that brief window of space, he remembered something his aunt Felicia, the wisest of his five aunts, had told him once—"When someone takes their time responding to your question, they are usually coming up with a lie."

"At my age, I've tried just about everything once."

They walked up to another piece—another Black man, thin, lithe body. His toned arms were extended like a ballerina and he wore a tutu.

"I find myself wondering—what does she want with me?"

"My mother has a thing for the Black male form. Call it curiosity, attraction, call it lust. She finds it fascinating. You should sit for her as long as she'll have you. As you know, she pays well. As you might not know, she can be a genuine bitch to sit for. But hey, at the end of the day, you'll have some extra money and you'll be immortalized like old Felix here. Maybe you'll be in a gallery one day."

Muriel worked in clay that would be fired in a gas kiln up to about 2,150 degrees Fahrenheit. To achieve immortality, he would have to be baked in an oven—not an image he enjoyed. The idea of sitting for her intimidated him, but he could absolutely use the money. That was how it all really started.

Two

"Don't move your hands so much! Quit blocking the light! Only talk when I start a conversation! I swear, this shouldn't be rocket science!"

That was how Muriel often talked to him. Barking her demands as he sat on the stool in her studio, which always seemed too hot or too cold. He would never have let any of his friends talk to him the way she did. If the money weren't so good, he would have quit early on. But the money was good. Capitalism was a bitch. And truth be told, he was intrigued by many aspects of the process. He'd never had much reason to come to Manhattan before—a few trips every now and then to a soul food restaurant in Harlem that his mother loved—and now he had a standing appointment there twice a week, in the type of apartment he'd never imagined existed. Central Park West was the opposite of Bedford Stuyvesant. The former was full of sunlight, status, privilege, and freedom. The latter conveyed shadow, repression, desolation, and violence. He could easily live where she lived, but she could never live where he lived. The wealthy, he was learning, had limits—were crippled in their own way.

He usually sat for three or four hours at a time. Their first session, they barely said a word to each other, she just gave instructions and sat there in her khakis and apron. At the beginning she sketched him on a huge pad. He just sat there, in the position she ordered, and focused on recalling the first times they had met. The old lady often came into

Comforti's for Friday lunch, and she always took the same seat in his section, a creature of habit. From the moment he first approached her, he noticed a distinct aroma about her—medicinal soap and overpowering tobacco. Rashid was a smoker, but he, like most people, tended to blow smoke away from himself. Muriel didn't seem to give a damn. The smell of cigarettes clung to her clothes like mildew. He and the other waiters guessed she must be seventy, eighty. She looked elderly, but not fragile. She tipped well, but there was a price to pay for it. She was malicious. Rachel called her "rancorous."

"Calamari, not too crispy! The cabernet sauvignon. But not the dry one like last time!"

The first time she brought Rachel with her, he could overhear parts of their conversation, and he realized she spoke to everyone in that tone. It erased any notion he had that she disliked him in particular. It wasn't he whom Muriel Auslander disliked. No, it became clear—the old lady hated humanity. He watched her seethe as she read the *New York Times*, which she did on every visit. Sometimes he heard her mutter with acid on her tongue about the ridiculousness of Israelis and Palestinians, the evils of the caste system in India, and corruption in governments all over Africa and Latin America. He wished that he could reach her, make her feel better somehow. Once he tried to tell her a joke, but his delivery was awful, and it fell flat.

"Buddy, you're no Richard Pryor, okay? Just make sure the cheese is warm on my manicotti this time. Last time it was like a fucking sponge."

"I know she can be overbearing at times but, please, cut her a little slack." Rashid was with Rachel at her favorite East Village cocktail bar. She was wearing the same powder-blue dress she had worn the first time they'd made love. It had a U-shaped plunging neckline that revealed her cleavage in such a playful and delectable manner that he would never see the color powder blue again without feeling instantly romantic. But Rachel's tone was serious, talking about her mother. "Her earliest childhood memories are of being on an overstuffed train heading to Birkenau."

"Birk—"

"It was a concentration camp. You know Auschwitz?"

"Of course I know Auschwitz." He stated this with a bit of impatience in his voice. He had only known her a little over a month, but he already noticed there were times when she took a slightly condescending tone with him. Sometimes he resented her for making him fall in love, but not often, and never for long.

"Well Birkenau was like Auschwitz's less popular sister camp. My mother never saw her parents again after they arrived there. If you look, she has a tattoo on her right arm—115342. My brother and I used to joke that we would play those lottery numbers constantly once we were old enough."

"Doesn't sound like a very funny joke."

"You had to be there. There's humor to be found in everything, my friend. *Ev-er-y-thing*. Would you believe she has never taken the subway in her life? She can't. It triggers her. Claustrophobia sets in. She taxis and buses it everywhere."

"That definitely explains a lot."

"You'd like to think so, wouldn't you?"

"What do you mean?"

"I mean there are a lot of Holocaust survivors who aren't miserable bitches. Sometimes it's just in the genes."

In the lobby of Muriel's apartment, the doorman, an affable older Black man, had called out to him as he exited the building.

"She a piece of work, Ms. Auslander, ain't she?"

"Yeah, you could say that. You know her well?"

"Known her for about twenty years. She's a diamond. You just have to wipe away a lot of coal first."

Rashid had never proactively listened to classical music his entire life. If he ever came across the genre, it was in a movie or on a television show. Rachel changed all that. As they sat in a hotel bathtub together, after hours of shared passion, she'd play Wagner's *Tristan and Isolde* over the stereo. He didn't love it and he didn't hate it, but with her it felt like he was receptive to anything. When he walked out of the hotel and into the warm August night, he pledged he would listen to more of "this Wagner dude." She had advised he start with Tchaikovsky.

It was always hotel rooms with Rachel. She didn't live in New York City. She lived in Boston, where she was a prominent flutist with the Boston Philharmonic Orchestra. She was also the mother of two children, an eight-year-old and a ten-year-old. She was up front with Rashid from the start. Her husband was a professor of music history at Boston College.

Rashid had never thought he would be the lover of a woman nearly twice his age. He had never thought he would be the lover of a white woman, a Jewish woman, a married one at that. But almost from the start, he was in it, alright. Rachel was on his mind more than he ever imagined a woman could be. And it wasn't just that making love to her exposed him to a new kind of unbridled euphoria. His obsession was with much more than the sex. Rachel ripped him out of his element. She introduced him to new territories within his skin. Life had shown him it paid off to be guarded. Hell, it was oftentimes the key to survival. Rachel, by opening herself to him, by risking her own safety, had shown him there was beauty in letting walls crumble. Sometimes he wondered why she chose him.

It wasn't that white women were out of his reach. Before his job at Comforti's, he had been a waiter at a Greek diner in Flushing, and one of his colleagues there was a theatre student at NYU, a self-professed "hillbilly from Indiana," Sabrina. They had started having sex after the Christmas party, over a year ago. But once he'd left the diner for Comforti's on Arthur Avenue, they'd lost touch. He had missed the way she said, "Jesus and Mary!" after she came, and the way, after they watched a Rolling Stones documentary in her dorm room, she often sang to him in a mock Jagger voice lines from their favorite Rolling Stones song as they passed each other on the diner floor.

Rashid thought he knew a lot about women, about how to give and receive. Ever since junior high school when he lost it to Yolanda Ramirez, he had felt pretty confident that he had what it took to be an adequate, competent lover. Yolanda had taught him lots of things, like that when the time was right, she preferred to be on top, "riding that shit like Seabiscuit." She had told him to slow down when he was pumping too vigorously and how to ease into it. She let him know when he was squeezing her tits too hard and when he was nibbling on her shoulder too softly. And he took it all in like the decent pupil he was. But when Yolanda seemed to act like she didn't know who he was in the school cafeteria days later, he became self-conscious. Feelings of inadequacy swam through him. He confronted her on the staircase and made it clear he wanted to see more of her, but she was candid. "I'm just not feeling you like that, Rashid, damn!" From that point on, he needed a woman to make it clear she desired him. Very clear. With Rachel Pollack that was never an issue.

With Rachel he became supremely aware that the body was an archipelago of sounds, senses, warmth, and textures. She was like a conductor. Sometimes she slowed him down, sometimes she sped him up. Sometimes she pulled from him a pulsating throb that needed coaxing to bring him to full crescendo. Other times she caused surges, ebbs, and induced tempos that led to compositions he could not have known existed within him. The best part was that their relationship was a give-and-take. Some days he wielded the baton, some days he manipulated the strings. He had never looked so forward to seeing someone as he did Rachel. It scared him the way his chest convulsed during moments with her. This type of intensity had been missing with other women, and he wasn't sure why this time it was so different. He couldn't help wondering if the allure of this feeling was similar to the high his father had felt from the drug that killed him. The affair and his intense devotion had all happened so unexpectedly.

After his third session with Muriel, Rachel had shown up at the apartment with her two kids for a "weekend in the city with Grandma." As the kids got settled into their room, she offered to walk him downstairs, claiming she had to stop at the store. In the elevator ride down, she looked him straight in the eyes with the intensity of a bird of prey.

"Honestly, how is she treating you?"

"She's treating me fine. She can be a little rough at times."

"A little rough? You are a good guy. I could tell the minute I met you."

"I'm not that good, trust me. She pays well."

"You have to let me buy you a drink. After all you've put up with, it's the least I can do."

"You don't have to do that."

"Come on. She and the kids will spend hours watching videos and shit. You'll be doing me a favor. I could use some adult time. There's a new bar on West Ninety-Sixth I've been wanting to try."

At the trendy bar, Rachel revealed a lot. It wasn't that she was drunk—tipsy maybe—she was just unusually open. He could not recall ever meeting anyone as direct as her. They would have a martini, step out and have a cigarette. Have a martini, step out and have another cigarette. By the third cigarette, he trusted her, felt comfortable around her.

Rachel's husband, she told him, was a genuine lecher. He had recently had an affair with one of his students, his third that she knew about in as many years. Two were with students; another was with a fellow staffer. They had tried marriage counseling, but she had serious doubts it was doing any good. In fact, she knew it wasn't. It was all for show. Her husband had always been a womanizer, even when they were dating in college. She thought marriage would change him. She thought marriage would change her. She called herself a fool.

"He needs to know—I need to make it clear to myself—he's not the only one who has needs, desires."

The time seemed to race by as they sat at the bar; it was like a sanctuary of sorts. When it got dark, they both realized she needed to get back to her mother's place. She insisted on paying for their drinks. At the entrance to the subway station, she touched his arm.

"What would you say, Rashid, if I told you I hadn't had an orgasm in four years?"

He raised his eyebrows and put his hands in his pockets as a crowd of passengers streamed out of the station, framing him, the taller, younger brown man, and her, the slightly smaller, older woman with the complexion of a faded dandelion.

"I would say that is a real shame."

"I would agree with you. Are you free Sunday afternoon?"

Three

His neighborhood, Bed Stuy, was the type of place very few ever had the opportunity to leave. Forward progression was not really a concept there, where the projects shot out of the ground violently like mighty oaks and surrounded the residents, densely packed into their tiny, cluttered, poorly heated rooms and hallways, in a protective shield of concrete and crushed glass. They called it a "trickle down" when reporting an upstairs neighbor's radiator leaking through the ceiling.

Some people did manage to leave. Darnell was currently living at Rikers. In retrospect, even Darnell would admit that it was a bad idea for him to shoot Jesse Reyes on the front steps of his own building in broad daylight, especially since Jesse clearly saw him and was expecting him. It also would have been smarter in a sense for Darnell to actually kill Reyes, not just shoot him in the shoulder. "But that's Darnell for you," his mother lamented shortly after his conviction. "Never could do much right."

His father had managed to leave too, but in the least preferred way. He departed Bed Stuy with a needle dangling from a crater-shaped vacuum in his left arm, while sitting on the scummiest sofa in the dirtiest basement of a shitty crack den that had once been a church. Yes, the Lord Himself had been present in those halls. Why *He* had left was anyone's guess. He probably got tired of the hopeless monotony. Or maybe He hit the numbers, moved down south, bought Him a house in Atlanta.

Either way, Rashid and his mother were alone, and it worked out well for both of them. She left for her MTA job at around eight in the morning, was home by six. He left for the restaurant around three, was home by eleven, midnight on weekends. The only time they ever really had to interact was on Sundays, preferably during basketball season. His mother had a tendency to walk around the apartment in a loosely tied boxer's robe that revealed the low-quality lingerie beneath it.

"Shid, I thought I asked you to bring me back some of that chicken parmigiana."

"We didn't have any extra last night, Ma."

"Well shit, you had to have extra something. I ain't picky."

"You said parmigiana. Anyway, I wasn't coming straight home. Didn't want to be holding leftovers all night."

"Oh, you too good to hold your mama's leftovers? What, you was hanging with that Jamaican slut?"

"She's from Trinidad, Ma. And yeah, we went to Kingpin."

"Trinidad, Jamaica, same shit. Just make sure you using a condom, Shid. That bitch is always with some new hoodlum every time I see her."

"First of all, it's not like that, okay? I thought I made that clear to you. She was my homeboy's girl in high school. I'm just looking out for her on his behalf."

"Oh, so you a guardian angel now, huh? I'm just wanting you to protect yourself."

He smiled. The truth was there was no girl from Trinidad. He just liked it that his mother thought he might have a girlfriend on the side somewhere.

"Oh, so now I gotta go out and buy lunch 'cause you can't bring me what you get for free at work?"

"I'll go get you something. What you want, egg and bacon sandwich?"

"On sourdough, please. Blueberry muffin too."

He loved his mother, truly adored her, while in the same confounding manner, deeply resented her for not being something more; the paradox of the poor Black son. He blamed her for the fact that he had to grow up in a place like the Jefferson Lane Housing projects. He blamed her for their living on the twenty-second floor, where he was forced to take the urine-soaked elevator even on the hottest summer days. But worst of all, his mother exposed a primal weakness of his: his inability to articulate feelings. So, after Darnell had been sent to Rikers, he had often wanted to reach for her. He wanted to express a love for her in a way he was sure his father and brother never could. She deserved that much. He wanted badly to find the words to tell her how he felt, but it was harder than it sounded. Like a bird blinded by the scorched light of the sky, he could never quite find that path. It bothered him more than he could say. It took him years to realize that it might not be his fault alone, that poverty did things to you. Poverty coarsened you. Poverty turned flesh to bone. Poverty made it so that it was easy to like someone who looked like you, but so much harder to love someone who looked like you. Poverty could cause you to fear the reflection in the mirror, the shadow on the ground. It made it easier to accept a foreigner. To be loved by a stranger. Maybe that was why he appreciated Rachel so much. She was absent all that poverty brought to Rashid's community. With Rachel he didn't need words to express love. With Rachel he just needed hands, lips, tongues, rhythm, pulse, heat, texture. With Rachel, love was like music. It filled you by running through you.

At the deli, he bumped into Marlon, one of his oldest friends. The two had grown up together, gone to school together, played alternating point guards at Cleveland High School. Rashid had always been impressed with Marlon, even envious. Marlon had been a good student in school. He actually paid attention. Marlon read the *New York Times*, and he retained shit that most found mind-boggling. Marlon could tell you how the stock market and the Electoral College worked. Marlon could tell you about the sun's gravitational pull. He knew what caused rainbows to form. What Marlon couldn't tell you was how to parlay that type of knowledge into success or how to hold down a steady job. He seemed wholly uninterested in achieving the American ideal of success, for reasons he kept to himself.

"You going to Sugar Dick's party on Friday?" Marlon asked him as they both waited for their orders at the counter.

"Sugar Dick's having a party?"

"Hell yeah! The nigga's turning twenty-five, what you expeck? And his third baby mama is pregnant again. There gonna be numerous reasons to light it up."

"Who's his third baby mama? Kaylee?"

"Shondra."

"Shondra? She wanna have another baby after what he put her through?"

"Never underestimate the power of some good dick. Same could be said for some good pussy. Speaking of—you still seeing that white bitch, the flutist?"

Rashid hadn't meant to tell anyone about Rachel, but pride overcame him and he needed to share her with someone. Marlon was one of the few people in his life that he could trust to not be judgmental.

"We're just hanging, man, that's all."

"Yeah, that's what you saying today, but I'm telling you—that white pussy gots power. Don't you remember *Othello*? That hit drives a nigga crazy. Make him do things he know ain't right."

"How you know about some white pussy? You ain't never even had none."

"Don't need it. I got two Asian bitches. That equals four white bitches."

"Shit, Zelda is barely Asian."

"Bitch is one-third Filipino. Stop showing your ignorance!"

At the Fulton Street subway stop, Rashid liked to indulge in a game that he'd played for over a decade—count the rats. He would stare down at the tracks and watch them scurry. Unlike many of his friends, rats always had somewhere to go. He counted six before his train arrived. He boarded, humming Tchaikovsky's *Romeo and Juliet Fantasy Overture*. The seat next to a white woman reading the *Daily News* was open, but when he went to sit there, she spoke up.

"I wouldn't. A homeless guy was just sitting there. I think he took a dump."

He looked at the seat and looked at her, trying to size up whether or not to trust her. A Puerto Rican guy in full Yankees gear nodded at him. "It's true. The dude was rank."

He looked back at the white lady. She was smiling at him now. She had a winning set of teeth and was wearing a sharp-looking business suit.

"I wouldn't fuck around with you," she said. "My boyfriend's Black, straight up Nigerian."

The doorman at Muriel's building caused him a subtle angst that he could not identify. The man was kind and completely affable, but seemed to Rashid to be some type of distasteful throwback to a time when people tossed around the word "sambo" with ease. Unconsciously, he made an extra effort to befriend the man, who always held the door open for him as if he were royalty.

"Looks like the Knicks may finally have a point guard, huh?" he said as he walked into the spectacular lobby.

"Sir, for the sake of my mental health, I cannot continue to believe in them New York Knickerbockers."

Muriel was in an unusually talkative mood. He wondered if he was starting to win her over. He was standing in the corner of the room, stripped down to just his underwear and socks. Her hands were working the sketch pad with a fierceness he didn't know a woman her age was capable of.

"How long have you been at Comforti's anyway?"

"Close to two years."

"How did you get started there?"

"That's actually a funny story. I used to be a student at Bronx Community College. A couple of business courses. A marketing course. I thought maybe I'd be a hip-hop producer."

"You people and that hip hop. My son loves it. I can't fathom why."

"There's actually some great stuff out there, the stuff that's not pop."

"Go on. You were saying how you got to Comforti's."

"Yeah, so one night we had this brutal snowstorm, maybe you remember, a couple years back in early December? It started around four p.m. Dumped about a foot by seven. They let us out of school early. I was heading to the subway station when I heard this lady just crying, wailing. I look and it's Mrs. Comforti, the manager. She's sitting on the end of the curb. She had just fallen off the sidewalk and shattered her elbow. I never seen someone so discombobulated. So I hail a taxi and get her straight to the emergency room. I stayed with her for two hours until her husband could get there. They made me promise to stay in touch with them. They were really grateful."

"So, why'd they make you a waiter? Why not manager?"

"I'm no manager. I don't have that skill set. I'd be a terrible manager."

"You never know what you're capable of until you're thrust into the role. Don't underestimate yourself. I never thought I'd be a teacher. Look at me now."

"You teach?"

"Eh, I teach a class a couple of nights a week at Parsons. I used to do it more, but the older I get, the more I hate the commute."

"Yeah, well, you have talent. That gets you far."

"You're a real charmer, you know that? I noticed it the first time I went in there. I could see the way the entire staff was drawn to you. You pull people in. Is your father as charming as you?"

"He was once. He was."

"He's no longer with us? Sorry to hear that."

"That's okay. I'm cool talking about it."

"How did he go, if you don't mind my asking?"

"His demons got the best of him. My father loved three things—women, the New York Knicks, and heroin. A woman nearly killed him once. The Knicks broke his heart often. And heroin proved to be the nail in his coffin."

"Isn't that something? How that drug does that to so many? My son has a similar problem, and I wouldn't be surprised if he ended up with the same fate. And what's really amazing is, I don't know about your father, but my son has everything, the little shit. As the first Jewish son, he was treated like a king. And he squandered it on his little bebop jazz projects."

"Two professional musicians. That's gotta make you proud, no?"

"You kidding me? You never saw two greater ingrates in your life. I swear, may you never have children as cruel and self-centered as mine. I told my Marvin we should just adopt. Those kinds of kids are always gonna be grateful, appreciative. But no, his ego couldn't take it. He had to see his face in theirs. Marvin the Moron."

"Do you miss him?"

"Every day, like the desert misses water. He held all of this together. He was my rock. That fucking Osama bin Laden, may he burn in hell eternal. And I don't even believe in hell."

"She's the victim in everything. She's always been the victim and she always will be." Rachel was standing at the stove in her brother's Lower

East Side apartment, pouring pancake batter in a pan while Debussy played throughout the spacious kitchen. Her brother was in New Orleans touring with one of his bands. She was nude, her full breasts swaying as she executed the perfect pancake flip and the pan hissed. Her brown bush was a shimmering distraction, tucked neatly between her muscular thighs. He loved how carefree she always appeared, how trusting.

"'Muriel Auslander stood in a cold yet sun-filled courtyard in Poland and watched as both of her parents were walked off single file to the crematorium never to be seen again. And she would never see the sun the same way after that. Sunlight would always remind her that life was cruel and unfair, and that there was nothing blacker than the human heart.' I wrote that once in school for a report we had to write on one of our parents. She made me do it. I was probably in the third grade, and she made me write that shit."

"Don't you think you're being a little hard on your mom?"

"You have to say that. You have to say that because you're the kind of guy who finds the good in everything and everyone."

"Are you being sarcastic?"

She grinned at him and the brown in her eyes turned bright, reflecting the flame of the oven. The idea that any man didn't find her desirous was absurd to him.

"Do you mind if I ask—how did your father die?"

"Of course, I don't mind. My father knew numbers like nobody's business, was somewhat of a financial whiz kid. He was a consultant for Cantor Fitzgerald, and on the morning of September 11, 2001, he had just arrived at their office on the 102nd floor of the World Trade Center for a meeting. Fucking guy was always early to everything. My mother still has a recording of his last call. Once he realized that none of them were gonna make it out, he called her to say goodbye. He got the answering machine because she was in her studio working, and she never picked up the phone when she was working. She never forgave herself for that."

"Jesus, I'm sorry."

"What are you sorry about? You weren't flying the plane."

"Well, no, I mean, but seriously—"

"'But seriously' nothing. Don't apologize for things you're not responsible for. Problem with your generation, you apologize too much."

"My generation? You make me sound like some teenager."

"Does my guy like his pancakes thin or thick?"

"Thick, please."

"I could have guessed that. You are a man who appreciates texture and girth."

"Girth?"

"Yeah," she said, tossing a hip in his direction with a wink. "Girth."

"I try to appreciate it all."

"Oh trust me, honey," she said, taking a seat in his lap. "You succeed." She kissed him, took a sip of coffee from a cup on the table, and hopped up to turn off the burner. With the skill of a diner cook, she flipped the pancakes onto a plate that already featured two slices of toast and a couple of sausage links. "Did you ever think one month ago today that you would wake up this morning, have sex with a forty-two-year-old Jewish chick, and then be served breakfast by her?"

"I would have to say the answer to that is no."

"The lesson here? Life is thoroughly unpredictable. With every sunrise there lies new possibility. Do you own a suit?"

"Do I own a suit?"

"Do you own a suit?"

"I do. I own one suit."

"Bring it next Sunday. I got us tickets to the opera."

Four

What is it about the first kiss that never leaves the mind? The question hit him periodically when he spent time with Stacie, the adopted daughter of his uncle Otis and aunt Felicia. He and Stacie were extremely close, always had been. The two had shared a bond since childhood. But they should never have been cousins and they both knew it. They never addressed the trauma that brought them into each other's lives. Stacie's father, Clyde, like Rashid's uncle Otis, had been a professional basketball player, and the two men had been inseparable. But Stacie's father was a renowned alcoholic and a physically abusive man. One night, when Stacie was around three, he returned home from a late night of poker and womanizing, and an argument broke out between him and Stacie's mother. When Stacie and her older sister woke up the next morning, the house was swarming with police, and the parents that she had once known were both in body bags on the living room floor. Clyde had strangled his wife and then killed himself with a pistol. That was how Stacie and her sister came to be members of his family. Similar to a recurring nightmare, the alarming brutality at the root of their union would remain with them forever.

Rashid was now watching Stacie through the window of the bookstore she worked at four days a week. His cousin was many things: former Miss Black Newark, part-time model/commercial actress, enthusiastic child double-Dutch champion, former lead singer of the short-lived R&B group Mochaside, spelling bee champ. As he watched her, wearing a long caramel pencil skirt and auburn blouse and showing a customer the Black Sports Icons section of the bookstore, all he could think about was what could have been. Had she not been his cousin, he could have married Stacie Merryman. Up until Rachel came along, she had been the love of his life.

She was a year and nine months older than him, and he had never felt closer to anyone in his family than he had with her. They had shared their first kiss when he was seven. They were seated together in the back seat of a car. Uncle Otis and his girlfriend at the time were in the front seat, taking them on a trip to Baltimore where his girlfriend's parents lived. They had stopped at a gas station somewhere near Philadelphia, and the adults had left Rashid and Stacie in the back seat while they went inside the store. She had been asleep. Earlier that week the two of them had been watching soap operas together, and they had joked about the dramatic way the white people kissed one another. They were both curious about the act of kissing. How much was lips? How much was tongue? How did you keep the noses out of it? In the back seat alone with her, he devilishly leaned in and kissed her on the lips as she was coming to. At first, Stacie slapped his shoulder, but when she realized it was him, she pulled him in for a second kiss. Her mouth tasted like Reese's Peanut Butter Cups and Pepsi, and he could have kissed her forever had the adults not returned with a six-pack of beer, two meatball subs, and a carton of Pall Malls.

From time to time, Stacie and her sister would come over and stay with Rashid's family in the projects. Sometimes he and Darnell would go to Newark and stay in their spacious home. Whenever they could, he and Stacie found pockets of private space where they could keep playing at romance.

It all stopped when Stacie and her sister abruptly moved to Tallahassee for two years to be raised by their aunt. He missed her during those years and wondered if she ever thought about him. He doubted it. When she returned, she was a new young woman, full of attitude and ambition, and she treated him like the two had never shared desire together. For him, she set the standard for any woman in his life. But that was ages ago. As adults, the two rarely ever discussed their childhood. It was like the lost chapter of their history book.

She handed him coffee in a Styrofoam cup and the two sipped and caught up. They sat close together, knee to knee, the way all-too familiar lovers do. He was the only person in the bookstore. Almost no one ever came to the store on Tuesdays, which is why he always showed up then. All these years later and he still liked her to himself, like in the back seat of the car. She had a new hairstyle—it changed often—long cornrows dyed blonde going down to the top of her shoulders. She wore nonprescription bifocals, giving her the appearance of a physics professor. A diamond stud dotted her left nostril.

"I'm going to Los Angeles on Sunday."

"Oh yeah? What's up out there?"

"I'm auditioning for a pilot. It's about a bunch of college kids who discover a time machine on campus and travel back in time to solve mysteries."

"Sounds brilliant."

"Yeah. Hey, someone's gotta pay for these acting classes. I'm also gonna pitch a screenplay to a producer my teacher recommended."

"Your screenplay?"

"Yeah, I told you about it. The romantic comedy about the high school teacher and the bank executive."

"*Blue Moon over Harlem.*"

"That's it. I've gotten some really good feedback on it. People in class think it's funny. Only problem is they don't let Black people do rom-coms, you know?"

"How do you mean?"

"When's the last time you saw a Black romantic comedy? You haven't. Hollywood doesn't believe Black people meet cute and fall in love. For them there has to be a catch always. A drug angle or a gang angle. Hollywood can't just let Black people be."

"I never thought about that."

"Most people don't. They have fed us what they think we are, and for the most part, we've bought it. We need to be on the inside. In the production meetings."

"If anyone can get that done, it's you."

"I'm gonna try. I'll be taking a playwriting class in Manhattan once a week starting in September. I wanna start to workshop that one-woman show."

"Look at you. Can't stop, won't stop."

"Hey, as far as I know, I'm only going on this ride once in this form. Gotta make the most. What about you? What you been up to?"

"I do not have a one-woman show I'm working on."

"Keep it up. You'll be waiting tables until you're sixty-five."

"Hey, we can't all strive for greatness. Someone has to serve and clean up after all you artistic geniuses."

"Rashid, why did you stop going to school?"

He nodded to a middle-aged white male in a business suit who had just entered through the front door and was taking in the place. "You have a customer."

"He won't buy anything. He just likes my Black ass."

"Another fan?"

"Hey, when you got it."

The business suit came right over to them and looked squarely at her. If he even noticed she was with another man, it didn't show.

"I read that Langston Hughes essay you told me about." His accent was English or Australian, sometimes Rashid couldn't distinguish between them.

"And?"

"You were right—a truly brilliant fellow. I'm here to get more."

"You are? Go over to aisle four. I'll meet you there."

The business suit took off with a pep in his step. Rashid watched Stacie rise from her seat with the grace of a modern dancer. "I swear," she whispered to him, so close he could smell her coconut-scented lotion. "These old white guys will do anything for some young Black pussy." And then, she was gone.

It was funny just how curious he had become about Manhattan. He'd lived in the city all his life, but not once had he ever been to Central Park. He wasn't overly impressed with it, yet he was relieved to be out of the room that functioned as Muriel's studio. She had been having an artistic block and suggested they take a walk to get some air. For twenty minutes they had walked in silence; he knew she preferred it that way. The sky was aluminum foil gray, the air smelled like a thunderstorm. She led the way and signaled for them to stop and sit on a bench. She was mumbling to herself, as she tended to do sometimes. It always sounded to him like she was communing with someone not there. A strikingly handsome gay couple, a white man and a Black man holding hands and walking their well-coiffed poodle, drew his attention. Her voice surprised him.

"I was here that night."

"That night?"

"That night when that privileged preppy-boy prick murdered his girlfriend, supposedly during sex. It happened right over there. I was sitting on this bench. They probably walked by me. She never knew what was coming. The statistics show so often that the person who will murder you is someone you know. Someone you thought you trusted. She had no idea. Or maybe she did know. Better to go by the devil you know than by the cruel hand of randomness. When I'm murdered, I want it to be by someone I know."

The statement struck him as incredibly peculiar, and for a moment, he wondered if Muriel Auslander was in full control of her mental faculties. Perhaps the world she knew was taking its heavy toll on her. If he knew better, he would have walked away right then and never returned to her studio. The same way he would have never lit Rachel's cigarette. But he didn't know any better. He was simply being carried by the current, and this current had a tremendous pull he was no match for.

Lincoln Center was another world to him. Rachel had told him to meet her by the west end of the fountain, but he had never known directions like north, south, east, and west. They never actually fit into his life. He preferred you said things like "Meet me on the side with the bodega" or "Meet me across from the car dealer right next to the Sutter Avenue subway exit." To his annoyance, he had no idea what the west end of anything was.

His suit didn't fit him as well as it once used to—another annoyance. He hadn't worn it since Aunt Cecily's wedding three years ago, and even then, he'd barely fit into it. The shoulders of the jacket bunched under his arms. The pants tightened uncomfortably around his crotch. It was a miserable conundrum. His mother had laughed at him as he left the apartment. He had told her a lie—he was going to a party the Comfortis were throwing. Better that than admit he was going to the opera with his married Jewish lover.

The greatest disturbance came some five minutes after standing there in the spot he had designated the west end of the fountain. The sun was blazing hot, which didn't bother him so much. He was a huge fan of summer heat. The unnerving thing was watching the waves and waves of people passing him by on the way to the theatre and realizing that none of them looked like him. He was a New Yorker through and through. He had no genuine beef with white people. However, this particular strain of white person struck him as possibly the vanilla whitest he'd ever seen in his life. There was a delicate, somewhat manicured edge to all of them, even the ones who had chosen not to dress up for the occasion. He overheard conversations but had no idea what anyone was talking about. He doubted any of them had ever been to a Knicks game, much less a Mets game. They were Tavern on the Green types. He felt invisible in their presence.

He thought he would be angry about it all for the rest of the afternoon, but when he saw Rachel walking towards him, her long purple dress hugging every curve of her to perfection, well, the game changed. When he saw her huge smile that made it abundantly clear just how happy she was to see him, every scintilla of angst left him and was replaced by desire and simple gratitude. He knew that even if he lived to be a hundred and twenty, he would never forget this image of Rachel Pollack, in purple, moving through the masses on a blistering afternoon, walking over to take his hands and say, "Well don't you clean up nice."

The opera was called *Tosca*, and he didn't understand one damned moment of it. He took in the spectacle of it all, from the way the usher led them to their seats in the balcony, to the way the orchestra warmed up, to the way the crowd applauded the conductor, to the spectacle of the opening curtain. He found it all rather overdone and ridiculously opulent. But he was also tremendously appreciative. At one particular moment in the second act, she reached for his hand and gripped it tightly. The language of the movement said to him, "Stay close, I need you to get me through this." He liked feeling wanted. He liked that she desired his presence. It all made him feel strangely . . . whole.

At the intermission, as he waited for her to return from the restroom, he noticed another Black gentleman across the floor, in a much nicer suit than his, having a glass of wine and taking in the scene. He could have sworn that he recognized the man from somewhere. He was a newscaster or something from the local TV news program. He was certain of it. He hoped to catch the man's eye and maybe make a connection, but the man never looked his way. When Rachel returned, she, too, had a glass of wine, and she offered him a sip.

"Hang in there," she said, sensing he wasn't really enjoying the experience. "Things really heat up in act 3."

He spent the final act as he had done the first two: fantasizing about returning to the hotel room with Rachel and peeling her out of that purple dress.

On the subway, heading back to her hotel room after sharing a pizza and beer in a new restaurant right off Columbus Circle, he could smell the garlic in her hair as she rested her head on his shoulder. It felt good to be with her that way. For a brief moment they looked like every couple in love in America. Their reflection in the subway poster was innocent.

"When did you first know you were attracted to me?" he asked.

"Who says I'm attracted to you?"

He enjoyed that side of her, playful, a little rude. Aside from Marlon, no one in his life made him laugh. He realized it was nice to be able to kiss the person who made you smile. She clenched her fingers tighter around his, as if she wanted the entire train to know he was hers. It flattered him, what this woman wanted the whole world to know.

"Whatever."

"It was early, very early. Like a few minutes after you walked away to get our drink order. You had a composure about you that I appreciated. A refinement. And I liked how you were with my mother."

"How was I with her?"

"Light. Unintimidated. Natural."

"You make it sound like being around your mom is hard."

"I only ever brought one guy home to meet my mother before Michael. He was a violinist and we had met my sophomore year. He couldn't stand my mother. He said he felt her judging eyes on him the moment he walked in the door."

He found his eyes wandering over to a couple standing against the sliding doors, holding one another close—a well-dressed older Black man with a salt-and-pepper Afro and a white woman in yoga pants and a hoodie, young enough to be his adult daughter. He wanted to know how they came to be together.

"Do you think your mother has judged me?"

"Doesn't everybody judge everyone?"

"I don't think I judge people."

"Oh really? You are the special one, huh? Time will tell."

Her warm lips kissed his neck and he couldn't help but grin.

"How do you think that couple over there met?" He nodded in their direction and admired the inquisitive look on her face as she scrutinized the couple.

"Hmm. Good question. Good to know I'm not the only one robbing the cradle on this train. He is an African American History teacher at Baruch College, and she was his TA for a semester. He has a wife and a kid at home, but he feels like his wife doesn't really appreciate their sex life anymore, she's become so engrossed in raising their son. He and the TA hit it off over grading papers late one afternoon in his office, and the two decided to have a drink at the local bar at the end of an exhausting day. Over a couple of martinis, she told him how she admires the way he carries himself in class, and she let it slip she always had a thing for confident, older men. He told her that he knew she was going to make a great teacher someday and that he appreciated how alive she made him feel. She blushed at this, and before you know it, they were making out in the dark booth in the corner of the bar. He left his wife for her, she left her boyfriend for him, and they now share a studio apartment in Crown Heights."

"You know, if this flute thing doesn't work out, you have a career as a romance novelist waiting for you. How did you come up with that so fast? Did you fall for your history teacher?"

"No, I fell for my waiter!"

Back at the hotel, he took extra care to appreciate her, gently caressing her collarbone with his fingers, suckling each breast, treating each nipple like a delicacy. They briefly fell asleep, but around three a.m., he leaned over to her figure and placed his lips sweetly on her warm, fleshy shoulder. His tongue worked its way up her neck to her ear, picking up a mixed bouquet of perfume and sweat. She turned to him, clearing her throat, and humorously said, "Again? My, what has gotten into you tonight?"

"Must be all that Puccini," he replied, as she mounted him. In the dark of the Ritz-Carlton, it was impossible for either of them to see the color of their eyes. The purple dress sat on the floor, shining in the moonlight like a silk eggplant.

Five

There was no oxygen in the space. He was racing to reach the surface, but he knew he would never make it in time. His arms, strong on the basketball court, were light and stringy like noodles under the immense pressure of the weight of the ocean. Drowning was certain. It was always certain, and yet he always woke up just in time. He gasped, bathed in sunlight from the hotel window. He looked over for Rachel, but she wasn't there. Only the scent of her, a body print in the sheet, and some blood spotting. Had he been too rough?

He heard a toilet flush in the bathroom, and she emerged, naked and on her phone. She was hostile, arguing with the only other person it could be—the husband. Something to do with their kids. He cobbled together a scenario from bits of stolen conversation: The husband had expected her to bring the kids to soccer practice on Friday. She had told him she had to be in Chicago for a recording session. Fury followed. She was a different person when she spoke to him. Her face drew taut, the color of an open blister. Her arms danced in the air like an incensed juggler.

"Jesus Christ, Michael, what part of 'I have a life too' don't you fucking understand? When you were knee deep in your thesis, I gave you space. When you had your monthly poker game with the Spellman boys, I gave you space. When you were fucking your Argentinian student, I gave you space. Now I'm demanding my space."

The rest of the morning would be tainted, he knew it. At breakfast they were quiet. She had a look in her eyes like she was trying to figure out if it was possible to get away with murder. He nibbled at his cranberry scone, sipped his coffee, wanted a cigarette. He noticed she was staring at him, seething a little.

"Where do you think all of this is going?" The purple dress was folded neatly in her bag, replaced this morning by black slacks and a floral-print blouse.

"I'm sorry?"

"You said something last night, and I'm just concerned."

"What did I say?"

"You said, 'I love you.'"

"I didn't say that."

"Are you calling me a liar?"

"No, I think you misunderstood me. I may have said, 'I love when you do that.' You do a lot of things that I love in bed."

"Is that so? Well, just see to it that you never say that to me, okay? The last thing we need is to be falling in love."

"Heaven forbid."

"I'm serious. What we have now is perfect. It meets both of our needs beautifully. Let's not go muck it up with all of these feelings."

He watched her sip at her coffee. It was like he was watching the ghost of the shadow of his lover from the night before.

"Did I hurt you last night?"

"What?"

"Did I hurt you last night? There was blood on the sheets this morning."

"I don't know if you are aware of this, but about once a month, us ladies—"

"Okay, okay!" He shot up and his chair fell back. He reached for his jacket pocket and fumbled with his pack of cigarettes. "You know, I'm not some dumb-ass nigger."

As he dropped the pack on the floor, she jumped at him. Grabbed him from behind. Stroked his shoulders. Kissed the back of his neck. Leaned her head on him. He closed his eyes, grateful. Somewhere in his brain he was starting to realize it would be smart to leave all of this behind and make this their last rendezvous. But of course, it was too late. What had started as something light, an interesting diversion into another world, was turning into something more serious. Maybe he *had* said he loved her. Rachel was on his mind most of the waking day and a large portion of the dreaming night. At work one afternoon, he had caught himself doodling her name on a napkin. He pretended it was all just for the great sex. For god's sake, he was humming Puccini on the subway.

A few nights later, after closing at Comforti's, he sat alone at the tiny bar, drinking a glass of scotch and watching Lucia ring up the receipts at the register. She was tapping the keys to the beat of the song on the radio, a pop classic. There was a fluidity to the woman's movements that he admired. If she hadn't managed a restaurant, she could have been a bullfighter.

"Mrs. Comforti?"

She turned to him, beaming. "I knew it. I could tell you had something on your mind, son."

"I was just curious."

"You are always curious. It's part of why I adore you. What is it this time?"

"I was just wondering—what do you think your life would have been like if you had not ever met Antony? Do you think you could have been just as happy?"

"But what a question is this? It is impossible to know for certain. But I assume, yes, I would have found a way to be happy. It's what we all have to do, no? Move to the light."

"I suppose. I wonder—how did the light become the light, you know? I mean who was it that established we should move to the light and not to the dark? What makes the light so much more appealing than the dark?"

"It seems reasonable, no? We all love a bright, sun-filled day. We are all afraid of the dark."

"And when people are dying, they always say—look to the light. Look to the light."

"Whatever has gotten into you, son? Are you in love?"

"Maybe. Maybe. I just wonder—if all the stars were black, and the night sky was ivory, would we recognize the moon?"

"Oh my, you *are* in love. It has finally happened. Love has reached our Rashid."

He looked at her, certain he must be blushing.

"I wish someone had warned me."

"Warned you of what, son?"

"Warned me that love—genuine love—is a lot like a fire."

His mother was not a religious woman. Never had been, never would be. The two times he had ever been to church were when he was a child, and he and his brother had been forced to live with his grandmother in Brownsville for a month. Their trip to grandma's seemed sudden, and it would take him several years to learn the true cause of it. A drunken Aunt Merna later told him, over her sixth Easter Sunday beer and Thunderbird, that his mother had been briefly incarcerated. It was over some indirect involvement with his father's drug running. Only the luck of an incompetent police filing had kept her from a much longer sentence.

His grandmother, unwilling to leave them alone in her home on a Sunday morning, had brought them to church with her. He had hated it. The images of well-dressed, sweaty Black folks with arms flailing, dancing around in spasmodic glee as they manifested the Holy Ghost— those images never left his mind. The Black church haunted him. The concept of a loving God escaped him. When he looked around the world at the way Black people were treated everywhere, from Angola to Zimbabwe, from Bed Stuy to Brownsville to Baltimore, he came to his own conclusion: *God must hate Black people and love white people.* The stark realities of the way both groups coexisted in the world were just too obvious to come to any other determination.

His mother had no time for ridiculous notions of sinners and saved, but she always said, "If there is such a thing as Heaven, Nat King Cole is singing there every single day."

He came home from his shift at Comforti's to his mother dancing alone in the living room to Cole's "Orange Colored Sky." She swept him up in her arms and they danced together. She was thick around the waist and, boy, could she move. There was an effortless energy about her dancing. When he was younger, men would ask for his phone number just so they could call his mother.

"I got the promotion!" she crowed.

"I didn't know you were in line for one."

"Boy, you never do listen when I talk, do you?"

They danced for two songs, and then she made them turkey and cheese sandwiches, which they ate at the table with cups of beer.

"Tomorrow don't come home too early from work. I'm putting down a few roach bombs and this place gonna need to air out some."

"You putting down a roach bomb again? Damn, you just did it a few weeks ago."

"And you see it didn't work. These motherfuckers are not playing. This one they told me is extra-strength. I need some of that shit they used on the Jews in them concentration camps."

Ever since they had seen that documentary on the Holocaust that rainy afternoon several autumns ago, his mother would make references of that type. It hadn't meant anything to him in the past, but now he saw flashes of Muriel, looking pained at her easel, glum as she sipped a mug full of chamomile tea at the kitchen table, her hand shaking as she smoked a cigarette.

"That's not funny, Ma."

"It wasn't meant to be funny."

"I'm just saying—sometimes you don't have to say a thing just 'cause you're thinking it."

"Excuse me?"

"Holocaust jokes, not funny."

"Excuse me for living, Schindler's Pissed."

It was rare to see a call coming from Rachel so late in the night. He was standing on the subway platform, playing count the rats. It was shortly after eleven, and he still had on his waiter's uniform. With some degree of concern, and the whisper of euphoria often associated with her, he put the phone to his ear.

"I know it's late. I just wanted to tell you—I owe you an apology."

"How do you mean?"

"You know what I mean. The last time I saw you. I was snarky, churlish."

"Churlish?"

"I wasn't kind to you. I've thought about it all week. I talked to my therapist about it."

This was news to him. He had no idea that she even saw a therapist, though it didn't surprise him.

"You talked to your therapist about me?"

"Yes, yes, I did. And I'm most likely projecting. I think the real problem is not that I don't want you falling in love with me. I think the real problem is that I'm the one falling in love with you."

Her words drenched him like a warm July rain. The subway platform dissolved. No woman had ever said those exact words to him before. He'd thought that perhaps these moments were only the made-up stuff of silly romantic comedies—a world supremely inhabited by white people. But the fact that Rachel was saying those words to him now, and that she had called him at this time, it affected him. This must mean that in some way she needed him. No one in his life needed him. In this act, there was something extremely precious.

"You think you're falling in love with me?"

"That's what I said."

"You really know how to take a man's breath away, Ms. Pollack."

"Don't make light of this. I'm back from Chicago on Tuesday morning. Can I see you that night?"

"You can see me whenever your heart desires."

"Good answer."

On the basketball court, a different side of him came out—a more cutthroat and competitive person took possession of him. He hated to lose, and he had low tolerance for any who didn't share his competitive zeal. On this afternoon, Marlon had to push Rashid off the court after his team lost a tight match to four Puerto Rican guys from Red Hook and he confronted the skinny man who had led them in scoring. The heavily tattooed man with a baby face had fouled him hard on the way to score the winning basket. There was blood trickling from the left side of Rashid's lip.

"That shit was a charge," he spit out over Marlon and another man who held him back.

Babyface sneered and waited for a few seconds to see if he was going to step to him.

"You better keep walking, motherfucka!"

"Chill, Rashid. This ain't Jets and Sharks out here. You gonna die for real."

He dabbed at his lip with a T-shirt. "Ain't shit gonna happen to me. I'm a take that fuckin' *puta* out."

"Chill, nigga, chill. That nigga is part of 7-6-5 Tigres. You don't wanna fuck with them."

"Fuck 7-6-5, they on our court!"

"Our court? Check you out. You really are Darnell's little brother now, huh? Yeah, come on, let's go get some hot dogs. My treat."

He and Marlon double-fisted hot dogs while they leaned against a parked car. Half his mouth was sore.

"What got into me back there?"

"What you talkin' 'bout?"

"I wanted to kill that dude. I wanted to crush his fucking neck in, all over a basketball game."

"You an animal. What you want? Evolution only go so far."

"It's more than that, man. Animals kill out of necessity, to survive. A wolf is not killing a sheep because he cut him off hard on the way to the hole."

"I'm sure animals kill over petty shit too. We just don't know it. I'm sure somewhere out there, a wolf killed another wolf 'cause the nigga looked at his woman the wrong way."

"Man, that is some deep shit, Marlon. It's amazing you don't teach a sociology class at, like, Yale and shit."

"Ain't it, though? Them white kids ain't ready for this knowledge I'm set to drop. Speaking of, you still got your Desdemona?"

"My Desdemona?"

"Your white girl, nigga. You still seeing her?"

"Yeah, I'm still seeing her. Seeing her tomorrow night, in fact."

"So this becoming a regular thing, huh? She still married?"

"I feel like that situation is on the clock, you know? She just needs time to sort it all out." It sounded ridiculous as soon as it left his mouth, but there it was. Something had definitely shifted.

"Yeah? Then what?"

"What you mean, 'Then what?'"

"I mean, then what, nigga? She gets her divorce and you and she walk off into the sunset like Bogie and Bacall or what? What's the grand plan?"

"Fuck Bogie and Bacall. There don't need to be no grand plan right now, okay? We just enjoying each other. Can't two people just enjoy each other?"

"You could enjoy that white pussy 'til you ninety-five. Just make sure y'all on the same page, that's all."

"Oh, so now you're a relationship counselor too?"

"You ain't in a relationship. You fucking. Get the two straight."

Rashid fixed his eyes on Marlon, then looked away. Across the street a homeless woman was collecting cans in her shopping cart. He had known the woman for years, Sylvia Herrera. She used to work at the supermarket where he bagged groceries as a boy. Sylvia had invited him to her family's July Fourth picnic one summer, and he had played Frisbee all afternoon with her daughter, Aricella. At the time he thought he might marry Aricella someday. Her sweet features and the effortless way she caught the Frisbee and hurled it back at him were enough to win him over. But things changed fast when he was a child. Aricella's father got into trouble with the law and owed money to some debt collectors. He disappeared one day and was never heard from again. Shortly after, Sylvia lost any ability to take care of herself or anyone else. Aricella was sent to live with an aunt in the DR. It was all very sad, but it also made Rashid just a wee bit grateful that he had a relatively stable homelife.

"It's amazing sometimes what happens to people. What life does to people."

"What people allow life to do to them."

"No, for real, look at Sylvia over there. Wasn't that long ago she was having us over to her place and making us all big-ass plates of arroz con pollo, remember?"

"Yeah, I remember. That shit was good. She was good people. And her daughter was so cute. Had that little gap tooth."

"Aricella. I wonder whatever happened to her. You know, a couple of weeks ago, I was coming out of Pepe's and I saw Sylvia talking to herself on the corner, so I bought an extra coffee and doughnut and I went to give it to her. But, like, right as I approached her, I could hear her conversation. The shit was crazy, man. She was having like a full-on talk with herself about how fucked up it is that people don't take the apocalypse more seriously and how we are all gonna suffer for dropping the bomb on Hiroshima and Nagasaki. She kept saying, 'We all got Japanese blood on our hands! All of us! Smell the blood! Taste the blood! Your day is coming soon!' The shit was creepy, Marlon."

"No, I feel you. I've heard her saying similar shit. She's definitely off in some David Berkowitz space. The sad part for her is there ain't no coming back. The human mind can only be pushed so far."

"How do we know that won't be us someday?"

"We don't. I mean, look at you—wanted to kill a nigga over a jump shot in your face twenty minutes ago. It's weird but, like, I think we underestimate this shit. Just how many of us are a hair's breadth away from losing all of our shit at any given moment."

"Don't get carried away. I restrained myself."

"Did you? I'm just saying passion is a bitch."

Six

He liked to rest his lips in the space below her right breast. It was always warm and smelled of sweat and lotion. With his head there, he could listen to her darting heartbeat. She often twirled her fingers around his ear and along his shoulders. "How did you get this?" she asked, looking at the scar above his right scapula.

"That? I'd rather not say."

"Oh, come on. How bad could it be? It looks old."

Her finger was gently on the scar now, both caressing and probing. Images flashed in his mind of blood, of his mother screaming, of Darnell leering. A decision that they shouldn't go to the emergency room.

Rachel's lips were on his forehead, then above his nose; they brought him back to the present.

"Come on. If you tell me, I'll give you the present I brought for you."

"You got me a present?"

"Maybe."

He had grown to adore that mischievous glint in her eyes. It made him wish he'd known her when she was a teenager. The trouble they could have gotten into together.

"Let me go to the bathroom first."

When he came out, he found her in the hallway by the front door. She was wearing a checkered robe that clearly belonged to her brother. She held a white shopping bag.

"Is that my present?"

"I've got coffee for us."

In the kitchen she played the local classical music station and poured each of them steaming mugs of coffee. The room was late-August humid and he wore just his boxers. He was looking at pictures on the refrigerator. They were mostly of different cities her brother had played in. The brother was handsome, not in a movie star kind of way, but in that nerdy, jazzy kind of way. Rachel and he had the same cheekbones and forehead, but any resemblance ended there. In one picture, he, Rachel, and a young woman their age stood outside Buckingham Palace, each flanking a guard.

"I bet your brother gets laid a lot."

"I'm sure he does alright for himself. Like me, he has low standards."

She was behind him now, rubbing his stomach.

"He was doing a semester at Cambridge then, and I was visiting him. It's funny 'cause he was dating a student there—I think she was a piano player—and another student, a French guy, took this picture of us. The girl, she was sleeping with both my brother and this French guy, and they both knew it. They were all cool with the arrangement. Anyway, she is like a super-high-level, A-plus student. She had lots of pressure from her parents to be successful. But she winds up getting pregnant, and as you can imagine, it's a mystery who the father is. I learned all of this on my last night there, when my brother and this guy are having this heavy talk at the pub about how to pay for the abortion. But she's freaking out because she's from a super Catholic family and abortion isn't something she can envision. So I'm back at school and I get a late night call from my brother, and he is just bawling, overcome with emotion. Turns out she did an Anna Karenina at the tube station, left behind a note apologizing to all of them for the disappointment she caused. My brother wound up coming home two weeks later. He wouldn't return to school again."

"An Anna who?"

"She killed herself. Jumped into the path of an oncoming train."

"What a terrible story."

"Yeah. I'm surprised he kept this picture. Audrey was her name."

Rashid stared hard at the picture now, focusing on Audrey's face. The woman in the picture didn't have the faintest idea that her days were numbered. That she was living on borrowed time. He had never known anyone who took their own life. He assumed mostly white people could do something like that—because they seemed to have a very hard time coping with pressure when the chips were down. Their lives had not prepared them for the crucible. It's why Rashid would never trade places with a white person if given the choice. They were a fragile, needy bunch.

He made a mental note to look up Anna Karenina.

"You gonna tell me about this scar or what?"

"Well, unlike you and your brother, me and mine are not very close. In fact, he gave this to me in an argument."

"Really? That had to be a serious argument. Let me guess—over a woman?"

"It was over his clothes."

"His clothes?"

"His clothes. I would wear them without asking him. He had much nicer clothes than me. His line of employment called for it. One time I wore his Adidas tracksuit out to a school event, and I got some pizza on it. The stain was hard to get out and he was pissed. He started out trying to strangle me. When that didn't work, he grabbed a screwdriver from the kitchen counter. If it had been a knife, I probably wouldn't be here."

"Jesus Christ, your brother has anger issues. Where is he now? You still live with him?"

"No, he's at Rikers. Will be for some time. He shot this kid in our neighborhood, a rival gang member. I was in the corner bodega buying Now and Laters and cigarettes when it went down. I heard the gunshots."

"Your poor mother. Did you know he was capable of that?"

"We all knew he was capable of it. Most of the kids I grew up with had to be. It's survival of the illest where I grew up. There's always someone wants what you got."

"You and I, we grew up very differently."

"You *think*? When we were in junior high school, my brother bet this other kid ten dollars that Mike Tyson would knock Buster Douglas out in three rounds. Ten dollars. Well, I don't know how much you know about boxing, but that didn't happen. Tyson got his ass knocked out. When that kid came to the school cafeteria the next day to collect, my brother didn't have the money. That kid called my brother a name, so my brother beat the kid with the school janitor's broomstick. Beat him so badly they had to call an ambulance to the school. Kid couldn't eat solid food for two months. To this day we still call him Jell-O. It's funny, and it's really not funny."

Rachel was staring at him now, a mix of concern and anguish on her face. She looked like she was trying to figure out the answer to a thousand questions, and they both were slowly realizing that the two of them could never last. They, too, were living on borrowed time. Life was the oncoming train. She went to the white shopping bag, which sat in the window, and she handed it to him.

"This is for you."

He took the bag. It was light. Inside there was a hooded sweatshirt with the Chicago Bulls logo on it. He reached in and, underneath the shirt, found a black box. The box was sturdy and polished. He looked up at her before he opened it. Inside was a small ivory-colored glass flute, delicate and beautiful. He carefully pulled it out. Her hand was on his shoulder now.

"It's handcrafted, Pyrex glass, fired in a kiln. It was one of the first flutes I ever played. My father gave it to me on my fifteenth birthday. It's got a limited note range, but it's magnificent for beginners."

"This is beautiful, Rachel. I can't take this."

"What do you mean you can't take this?"

"I mean it's too much. I don't even play."

"Well, that's the beauty of it. Maybe it will inspire you to start to explore. Maybe it will plant a seed."

"It's too precious. You should save it for one of your kids someday."

"Please. My kids are spoiled. They receive all sorts of gifts they never use. I really like this for you. The last time I saw you, I caught you humming Mimi from *La Bohème* when you were in the shower, and it just melted my heart. It made me think I'd really touched you."

"Did you have doubts before that?"

"No. Can you just take it, please? I shouldn't have to explain a gesture of affection. I would feel better knowing it was with you."

He put it to his lips and played a couple of odd notes. She clapped.

"Oh! My flutist of Bed Stuy!"

Seven

There was a purplish sadness about Muriel, and it weighed her down like plum cement. He noticed it the minute she gazed at him from over her easel. If there were a way that he could bring a smile to her face, he would have done it. He genuinely wished he knew how. But he also knew it wasn't possible. The old lady'd seen too much. In all likelihood, she was just waiting to die. In between meals, drinks, her art, she was expecting darkness. It was how she saw the world. Rashid watched her hand tremble a little as she held the brush. Her wrinkly, veiny hand had brown spots, tiny pools of decay on withered salmon flesh.

He wondered what it must have been like, the camp. The documentary he and his mother had watched showed grainy black-and-white footage of the bunkers. Emaciated bodies. The lines to the showers that rained down acid poison. What a nightmare. It was a testament to overwhelming human strength that she was there with him. He wanted to applaud her, to tell her that he appreciated her. But she made it impossible. It was difficult to even like her.

"What is going on with you?"

"I'm sorry?"

"You're fidgety like you've got fucking crabs in your drawers. Are you okay or what?"

"I didn't notice. I guess I just . . ."

"Fuck it. We're done today. We'll try again next week."

"I can do a better job of staying still."

"What part of *'Fuck it'* don't you understand?"

She tossed a couple of fifty-dollar bills at him like he was some homeless guy outside the bodega. The bills were wrinkly and he had to scoop one of them off the floor. She walked away and he heard her bedroom door close. It was not the first time she had entrusted him to see himself out. In the elevator was an older woman who smelled of baby powder and wore so much makeup she reminded him of an overused Barbie doll. Out of the corner of his eye, he saw her move her purse away from him to her other hip. It infuriated him. But when the door opened to the lobby, he nodded and signaled for her to walk first. He knew it was part of his responsibility to make white people feel safe in his presence.

Before he entered the subway, he stopped and leaned against a store window, pulling out his phone. He wanted to call Rachel, if only just to hear her voice. But what if she was at home having family dinner? Perhaps putting the kids to bed? Or maybe, just maybe, she was sitting on her porch with a glass of wine in her hand just hoping he'd call.

After their second time together, she'd had to race home because her son had a fever. She told him she wished she could have stayed in bed with him and that she could not stop thinking of him all night.

"I sat on the porch with a glass of wine, and the moonlight was so fierce and bright, I was afraid it was exposing all of my scars and wounds. It was like an X-ray into my soul, exposing every ripple your hands and mouth had put there."

Thinking of that, he called her and it went straight to her voice mail. "Hey, I was thinking of you. It's one of those moonlights tonight."

The next day, he shared the incident of the woman in the elevator with Marlon over pork dumplings and chicken fried rice.

"Shit, you sound surprised."

"I was surprised. No shit like that ever happened to me before. It's happened to you?"

"It's happened to you before. It's happened to every nigga. Your Black ass was too ignorant to see it, is all."

They both reached for the last dumpling, and Marlon stabbed Rashid's hand with a fork before seizing it.

"You are one ruthless Negro, Marlon."

"Remember Professor Kramer's biology class?"

"Nobody remembers Professor Kramer's biology class."

"I do. I'll never forget this one time he was telling us about penguins. It was fascinating."

"What was so fascinating?"

"I looked it up later just to corroborate it. You know penguins live in constant fear of the dark? Like, I'm talking terrified. They are terrified of the dark. You know why?"

"'Cause they can't see shit out in the North Pole?"

"First off, nigga, they don't live in the North Pole. They live in Antarctica. But yeah, that's part of it, of course. But more important, they are afraid of predators, predators that lurk in that unknown darkness. Mostly whales and leopard seals, but it's really the leopard seals. These seals just terrorize them at night. Those penguins have been known to just up and move entire masses to new locations to avoid the danger of being eaten by them. You ever hear of white flight?"

"Who ain't heard of white flight?"

"Okay then. It's really no different. White people fear us, man. They fear our Blackness. We represent the darkness to them. We represent potential danger. I remember when we were kids, my father was outraged about that story where a white dude got on a train, saw four Black kids surrounding him, and just started firing. He shot them all. And white people in this city cheered him on. They called him a vigilante. And it's because white people understood—that scrawny white man was a penguin, and when he looked out at those four Black kids on the train, he only saw leopard seals. In his mind it was kill or be killed. White people understand this."

Rashid played his flute all week. He was getting good at it—self-taught good. "Silent Night" was his favorite. The sound of the instrument brought a richness to his skin. In Stacie's bookstore, alone at the counter having coffee, she was intrigued.

"Where did you get that?"

"It was a gift."

"A gift from who?"

"A friend."

"A friend, huh? That Italian woman you slave for?"

"I don't slave for her."

"Whatever."

"You know, there is a very negative side to you, cuz. It worries me."

"Don't you worry about me. Any negativity I may have, you can bet is well earned."

"I came here to find out how your trip to LA went. You sell your script?"

"No, I didn't sell my script. You really think those tighty-whiteys in Hollywood know what to do with the type of story I want to tell? You think they really give a fuck about portraying Black lives as we know them? Hell no. They want their Blacks *Cosby Show*–style—educated and easy for Caucasians to digest. And if not that, then Shaft-like, one step away from Sing Sing. This cracker even told me, he said, 'I liked the characters and the pacing, but I kept wondering when we would see some real urban tension, ya know? Like where were the drugs, where were the gangs?' This cracker said this to my face, Shid. It's amazing. It's like, when they see us, they don't actually see us. They see either an idealized fantasy or a danger, a threat. We aren't three dimensional in their eyes."

"Man, that is so sad. You went all that way for nothing?"

"Pretty much, yeah. One of them told me they thought I had strong vision, wrote crisp dialogue. He said he'd pass my info along to a friend in the television department. He said he might be able to get me some episodic work."

"Well, hey, that's something, right?"

"Yeah, but then five minutes later he tried to get in my pants as he walked me to my car, so I'm pretty sure that door got closed right after I slapped that hand away."

"You, my dear cousin, have too much integrity for that business."

"That's just the thing, it's not even that, I mean, I genuinely do not like white guys, zero attraction. But if he had at least looked like Robert De Niro or something, I might have let him, if I thought it would help."

"Come on, you do have some attraction to them."

"I'm not down with sleeping with my oppressor. It isn't appealing in any way to me. It's different for you brothers. You get with a white woman, it's like a source of pride or something. Like you sticking it to the Man, flaunting his worst fear in front of his face. But for us sisters, it's a different story. There's no bragging in it. We can't replace what was stolen from us."

On the subway he glanced at his foggy reflection in the window. He had on a new button-down shirt, pink, from the Gap. The candlelight in the club was so soft, it gave the entire place the look of an old movie. The crowd was well dressed. He sipped on his cognac and watched her brother's trumpet solo. He was onstage with a small five-piece band. The singer, a voluptuous woman with feline brown eyes and skin, could not have been more splendid. He wasn't sure why she was in that dive in the East Village. Sometimes his eyes met with the singer's. He wasn't the only brother in the room, but he was the youngest, and probably the best looking. He felt Rachel kick him under the table.

"Watch it. She knows you're coming home with me tonight."

It was sweet to him, the notion that she might be jealous. But lately he had started to seriously consider: Shouldn't *he* be the jealous one? She still shared a bed, a history, a life with her husband. The husband was the full meal. He was the table scraps. It caused a slow burn beneath the surface of his palms.

At the end of the band's first set, the brother came over and sat with them. Up close he was less attractive than he'd seemed in the pictures on his refrigerator. He was older, sweatier, his face was clean, but strained by what Rashid clearly recognized as years of heroin use—some version of the familiar bony, scab-ridden face of his long-gone father.

"My sister has told me a lot about you," the brother said.

"Hopefully not so much."

"I told you," she chimed in. "My brother and I share everything. We know where all each other's skeletons are kept."

"I'm glad to meet you. Michael's never deserved her."

Rashid felt awkward and just nodded. He watched as the two of them caught up on his travels, her family. The brother was off to Germany next, would be there through the end of the month. He envied the brother's lifestyle. It made him wonder if he would ever leave America someday. The brother got up to excuse himself, he needed a quick cigarette break before the next set. Rachel rose from her seat and joined him, bidding Rashid to stay back and keep their seats. For whatever reason, she didn't want him to join them. After they were gone he looked around at the attractive crowd, and he ordered another set of drinks.

When Rachel returned, there was something off about her, something he couldn't quite pinpoint, but he knew it involved more than just cigarettes. When the lights dimmed, she leaned into him and put a hand on his thigh. For a brief time, they were like a real couple; it was a sensation that he had felt in brief instances with her and yearned for more of. The third song in the set caused Rachel to coo, and she grabbed his hand and leapt from her seat. The two made their way to the end of the stage, where a tiny dance space sat empty. She took him in her arms and the two moved slowly together. He didn't recognize the song, but it was soothing and haunting. The chorus was *"Once in a blue moon, you will meet the right one. Once in a blue moon, find your dear delight one."* Before he knew it, several other couples had joined them on the stage. Rachel beamed at him.

"We're trendsetters," she said.

"This is a beautiful song."

"It's a Bernice special. Nobody slays this song like her. I can't tell you how glad I am you're here with me."

"I wish we had more time like this together."

Her finger met his lips. "Appreciate the now."

Years later, after all the clouds had subsided and moved on to haunt others, when Rashid thought he was safe to view the sun again, he would hear this song being played in a different bar, with a different singer, on another side of the world, and he would find the combustion process starting all over again. He would suddenly cry uncontrollably, every note pulling at every piece of him, reminding him that the past was never the past. Music could inflict suffering. He played that song whenever he needed to convince himself that sorrow and beauty were two sides of the same coin; it was okay for them to coexist. This song became a stark reminder that when times got too high, around the corner immense pain was patiently waiting to devour you whole. It was just one song, and it could undo months of healing.

> *Then with a thrill, you know that love is true*
> *Once in a lifetime, when the moon is blue*

Eight

In the nighttime, the visions came again to terrorize him. He would not have minded if they were varied and disparate; it was the predictability of the threat that frustrated him. In the dreams, he was always surrounded by water, immersed in it. Gray-black water. It was always pulling him deeper and deeper; he was always reaching until he was fortunate enough to gasp awake. The dreams were new, had only started when he'd become the flutist's lover.

Usually she grasped his hand, kissed his cheek, and brought him back to reality in her unique and treasured manner. But she wasn't always there, and she would never be in a position to always be there. He rose from his damp pillow, alone in the bed this time, and walked over to the window. Below him he saw the soft glow of the morning sun rising over Greenwich Village. Joggers and dog walkers passed by. A bodega owner was spraying down the sidewalk with a hose. He felt as if he were in a foreign country. He opened the window and sat on the sill with one leg outside, smoking a cigarette. The front door opened, and Rachel walked in, fresh and chipper, carrying two cups of coffee and a brown bag.

"Ah, good, you're awake."

"She comes bearing coffee."

"And blueberry muffins. There's the cutest place off Bethune Street. It's run by these two queens who are just hysterical. They should have their own TV show."

She sat across from him on the windowsill and opened both of their coffees. She pulled a muffin from the bag and gently ripped a piece off. He could smell the damp, rich blueberries. He enjoyed the delicate way she performed acts, like a dancer.

They sat in silence for a bit and just took in the city below over a shared cigarette. There was something about this time of day that always appealed to him. Even back in Bed Stuy, where so much of nature was tinted with a sepia-toned menace, it seemed to him that nothing could truly go wrong in this small frame of time when the city was just taking its first breaths and even the rats had retreated. She placed her leg on his lap.

"So, listen, there is a chance this will be the last time I see you for a few weeks. Maybe a month."

"Why is that?"

"I'm about to go into rehearsals on a new project. It's a film soundtrack, an indie project a friend of a friend recommended me for. I'm helping with the score."

He nodded. He hadn't yet imagined he'd go for such a long stretch without seeing her.

"So, what, like October maybe?"

"October is extreme. But maybe."

As he watched her eat her muffin in a manner he found a little too nonchalant, he felt the smallest surge of anger somewhere inside him.

"Well, don't sound too broken up about it."

There was another longer silence. He watched below as a mother with a baby tied to her stomach and a small dog on a leash walked up to the fruit stand and inspected the grapefruits.

"I do have responsibilities, you know."

"Yeah, I know. You have a whole other life. A husband, kids, probably a dog."

"That's suddenly news to you?"

"No, no, it's not news to me. It's just—"

"You knew I had a separate life from day one. We were both very up front about this."

"No, you're right. I know. I just think it's nice for you. You can just move back and forth between both worlds without a care, you know? Nice upper-class *Brady Bunch* life there. Nice young lover over here."

She leapt from the sill and walked into the other room. Out of the side of his eye he could see that she was feverishly changing clothes. He watched the mother below, who had dropped several grapefruits on the ground. He had the urge to go down and help her, but he just sat there sipping coffee he couldn't taste. Rachel walked back in, fully dressed, holding high heels in her hands.

"You think this is easy? Huh? You think this is easy for me?" He continued to monitor the mother below. He no longer cared to see Rachel. "You think after a night as lovely and precious as last night, you think it's easy for me to just get on the train and go back to that fucking man-child I have to deal with? Him and teacher-parent meetings and youth soccer. You think I don't want to just stay here all day and night? You're not ready for this. I should have known."

He watched her dance around the room, flipping things over, madly looking for something. Seeing her so furious, he began to think that perhaps he did matter to her. He rose and went to her. He grabbed her hands.

"I'm sorry. Okay, I'm sorry. Just the idea of not seeing you for a week is sometimes more than I can imagine." A surge welled up in his chest that was wholly new to him. It caused his voice to quiver slightly. "And every time you leave, I wonder if you will ever come back. And it scares me because I can't picture a life without you. I don't know how this happened, but I feel empty without you. Sometimes I wish I'd never met you."

And then she was in his arms and he was in her arms. Her wet cheeks on his neck.

"We let it go too far," he heard her say. "We let it go too far."

"I blame Tchaikovsky."

Now she was laughing, and it was the sweetest sound he assumed he would hear all day. The taxi ride to the Port Authority was quiet, both of them engrossed by their own realities. There was a vision he could not shake. He found himself playing out the scenario over and over, each time more perfect and disturbing. He saw Rachel returning home that afternoon, walking in the front door and her kids running up to embrace her. She would sweep them up in her arms. The husband would appear from the kitchen, wearing a cooking apron like the one he'd seen the Comforti's sous-chef wearing, but this one said, "Father Knows Best." The husband kissed her and told her she was just in time for her favorite dinner—lamb stew. They would all sit around the table like a scene from one of those corny holiday movies his mother loved to watch, and share stories of the weekend. It would be like he'd never existed, and it was that fact or absence that held the true pain—the dagger to his heart.

They walked to her gate hand in hand, and as he passed a store window, he took in their reflection, and it brought him an inexplicable joy. There was an indescribable beauty about the city, which he knew was absent in other places like the Midwest and the South, in that nobody appeared to care about them at all. They were simply two tiny splotches of paint on a huge, ocean-sized mural. The train wasn't ready to board, so they just stood there. She straightened the collar of his shirt.

"I understand you, you know. I was once the person you are now. I was in college. It was my first affair and my last, until now, I suppose."

"Who was it?"

"He was a professor. He was the head of the Philosophy department, and an unhappily married father of three. He was special to me, and I was to him. I kept thinking: *Someday he'll leave them. Someday I'll have him all to myself.*"

"It's selfish, isn't it?"

"Yes, it is. But it's also the most natural thing in the world. Especially when one is partially broken. And you and I, we're broken."

"How do you think I'm broken?"

"That is a question you need to ask yourself."

"How did it end?"

"Not well. When he finally, callously cut me off completely from his life, I acted out. I swallowed a whole bottle of sleeping pills with a half bottle of chardonnay. I wanted him to suffer. To feel remorseful for the rest of his life. Someday you will want me to suffer too. You probably do already."

"That's not true, Rachel."

"It's okay. I understand it. It's part of the process. When you love someone it's like you're placing yourself naked at the center of a raging fire. And the odds that you leave that place without being scorched alive aren't very good. I just never want you to hate me. It might be inevitable, but I never want you to hate me."

"You're being ridiculous now. I could never hate you."

"I've learned something about hate. You might be too young to know this, but when you take account of the people you hate today, there is a common theme—they are all people you loved yesterday."

He waited a week for her phone call, and when it didn't come, he sought her out in other ways. After sitting for Muriel one day, he went downtown to the tiny jazz club in the village where they had gone to see her brother play. The brother wasn't there, but the singer was. Her hair was styled differently, but she still had that achingly profound voice. Hers, he thought, was a life that had felt its fair share of pain and heartache. No voice that penetrating could have been spared profound agony.

He sat for her entire set, but when she started "Once in a Blue Moon," he felt his throat tighten and he ordered a double. He sat at the bar and glanced over at their former table, where a new couple sat now. He remembered how it felt to dance with Rachel—his arm around her waist, the firm anchor of her hip bone, the scent on her neck, gardenia and cigarettes. He wondered if she knew—had any idea at all—just how she affected him.

On his fourth drink, he started to question how he could have let himself get in so deep. He knew better than that. His friends all saw how this would end. But he hadn't been able to keep it light, hadn't been able to keep himself from wanting more than they both could give. He wondered just what was it about her that was so special, anyway? The sex was great, sure, but was there really that much more to her—to why he felt almost desperate to keep her? Why did that song make him ache for her? Make him feel hollow inside? He bet Muhammad Ali never cried over a piece of ass. He bet Shaft and Reggie Jackson never cried over some woman who was clearly taken. He barely noticed when the singer slammed her purse down beside him at the bar and took the seat next to his. She turned directly to face him.

"Hey, hon, I remember you."

"I remember you too."

"You were here a couple of weeks back with Caleb's sister. Y'all got a thing."

"You could say that. Or we did."

"Over that soon, huh? Sometimes it's like that."

"I suppose. Hey, you have a stunning voice. Just beautiful. I love listening to you."

"Why, thank you, hon. You sweet. Where you from?"

He bought her a drink, a Tom Collins, and they talked her entire break. She grew up in New Orleans, where her father was a school principal and a preacher, and her mother was a registered nurse. She left New Orleans after high school and joined a girl group that toured with Al Green from time to time. She had a daughter three years older than Rashid, who was in the chorus of a Broadway show, and a son a year younger, in graduate school in Chicago. She proudly told him she was on her fifth marriage.

"You got to have a sense of humor about it," she said. "Each romance is like a building block. You just have to do your best to make sure you're growing with every one and not regressing. I know I am. I went from dating an emotional abuser to a physical abuser to a substance abuser to a con artist and now I'm with a doctor—a urologist. And each one, don't you know, I was madly in love with. Each one of them I would have laid down my life for. Each one of them served some greater purpose in my life. It's a funny thing, love. I didn't used to believe in therapy, you know how us Black folks be—therapy is for Jews. But I started seeing a therapist after my fourth marriage went kaput. I wanted to know, *What is it that I keep getting wrong? What is it about me that is attracted to these clearly incomplete men?* And I started to learn a little about myself. I was like nearly all of us—I was using love to fill some deep crevice inside of me. I was using sex to flood the darkness with light. I had to look at myself in the mirror and ask, What is it that we are doing when we reach out to love another person? What great gaping hole are we trying to fill? What was it that cut me so deeply that I will forever be trying to stop this bleeding? Why am I such damaged goods that I keep connecting with other, worse-damaged goods?"

"So, what led you to do so well with number five?"

"Honestly? I think I just got lucky."

Nine

When Rashid was eight years old, his mother got him his first pet—a green-and-yellow parakeet. He named it Woodstock, after one of his favorite cartoon characters. A bird was not like a dog or a cat, or even a hamster. You couldn't snuggle with it, cuddle it, take it on walks. At first, he had a hard time connecting with the animal. But that changed over a couple of weeks as the bird became familiar with him. When he would open the cage to feed the bird, it would playfully nibble at his finger. When he walked away from the cage, the bird would tweet until he returned. Once in a while, he would let it out of the cage, and it often landed on his shoulder. Woodstock became a companion and a source of joy for Rashid. Even Darnell, so moody and mean spirited, developed an affection for the bird.

One summer afternoon, Rashid had been scrambling eggs, and he burnt them so badly that he had to open the living room window to air out the place. His mother sent him to the store to buy groceries, and before heading home, he stopped to play video games at a local arcade. When he returned to the apartment, he immediately saw the open window, and he felt an eerie stillness that was very much out of place. He went to the empty cage and then scoured the tiny apartment for Woodstock, but the bird was nowhere to be found. He had forgotten that he'd let him out that morning. Sobbing, he went to the window and looked out at the vast panorama of housing projects all around him. In his heart of hearts, he knew he would never see Woodstock again.

"Can't blame him," Darnell said coldly. "That nigga saw a shot at freedom, and he took it. We should all be so lucky."

He lived with an emptiness deep in his gray soul for several days, weeks even. He told himself he would be careful to never love anything so much again, and he'd thought he had been successful in steeling himself against such unforeseen pain. He was wrong. The absence of Rachel in his life was far worse than any that he could have imagined. It was like surgery on the brain without any anesthetic. It was a persistent hum that sounded to him like the lighting of a match. On the subway, he stared hard at a woman who had the same physique and hairstyle as Rachel. Only when she looked back at him uncomfortably did he catch himself. He listened to Tchaikovsky more and more, and he kept the flute nearby, often in his coat pocket, though he didn't have the heart to play it. By early October he looked out the same window from which Woodstock had abandoned him, and he resolved that Rachel wasn't coming back either. Time healed nothing. He forged on.

He took his mother out for her birthday, to her favorite soul food restaurant in Harlem. Stacie and Aunt Felicia joined them, and they all laughed, sharing stories over barbecue ribs, ham hocks, beer, and martinis. Sitting there, surrounded by women he loved, he recalled that shortly after Woodstock had disappeared, his mother had done something. His mother had gone out and purchased a new parakeet for him. But she didn't tell him as much. She had gotten a bird that was nearly identical to Woodstock and she had lied to him, trying to pass the new bird off as Woodstock returned. She claimed he had just appeared on the windowsill one day, and for about half a day, Rashid had believed her. But it didn't take an ornithologist to tell that this new parakeet wasn't his old friend. This one had wider eyes, and though the same colors, the flecks of green on his wings were slightly off from its predecessor. He called it Woodstock but knew better. He never told his mother that he knew what she had done. Several months later the bird died of an unknown sickness, and that was it for him and pets. But he would never forget how his mother had tried her best to alleviate his heartache. It taught him that you could love someone and lie to their face because you thought it was what they needed to hear.

When his mother and his aunt got up to go to the bathroom, he and Stacie ordered another round of martinis and went out for a smoke. The sky was threatening rain, but it was warm out for the moment on 125th Street. She took the cigarette pack and lighter from his shirt pocket, placed two cigarettes in her mouth, and lit both of them. He looked on, enchanted at the sight of the firelight against her mouth.

"Hey, I wanted to ask you a favor while I'm not drunk," she said, handing him his cigarette.

"What's that?"

"Can you come over to my place sometime this week? I have been working on this Nina Simone musical, and I want to play a couple of songs for you. Get your feel for it."

"Nina Simone? I thought you were working on a play."

"This may sound hard to believe, but I can do two things at once."

"Does it have to be at your place?"

They both snickered. He did not like Stacie's roommate, a Cuban American law student with views that were annoyingly conservative.

"Minerva probably won't even be there. She's been spending a lot of time at her new boyfriend's place in Flushing. I wouldn't be surprised if she moved in with him soon."

"New boyfriend? What, did she dump Dick Cheney Jr.?"

"Apparently he was not ready for a committed relationship. Hey, speaking of, I have a new employee at the bookstore I think you should meet. She's a cutie, a sister just moved here from Detroit. Wants to be a chef, open her own five-star restaurant in Brooklyn."

"Ooh, a sister who can cook? Sign me up."

Just then his phone rang. He pulled it out and was surprised to see it was Muriel's number. He hadn't been to sit for her in nearly a month. He put his finger up to Stacie and answered the call. She was animated, told him she had had a great resurgence in recent days, and she wondered if he could get in to see her this Thursday. A small part of him wanted to say no, but he could use the money. And more salient, he knew it would be an opportunity to find out how Rachel was doing. When he hung up, his cheeks were flushed.

"Well, that call must have been special."

He didn't know how to respond, so he just smiled sheepishly and lit a new cigarette.

On the train ride home, he and his mother sat side by side, knee to knee. She held a large take-out bag in her lap that smelled like the South. They had sat in silence a long time, but he could tell something was on her mind. Eventually she cleared her throat.

"Your brother asked me to come and see him."

"Okay."

"I'm gonna go next Sunday." He nodded. He knew what was coming. "You wanna come with me?"

"No, Ma. No, I don't. How many times do we have to go through this?"

"I was just thinking—it wouldn't kill you to let him know . . ."

"Ma!" His tone was all at once brutal. He had forgotten what this type of rage felt like, the subtle toll it took on one to wear this much anger. "He doesn't get to do that."

"Do what, Shid?"

"He doesn't get to manipulate us into feeling pity for him. He tried to take that kid's life. He tried to leave a mother without a son. He doesn't get to do that." His mother spasmed, a whimper from the back of her chest that caused him to feel small. "I know you have this undying devotion to him, your firstborn and all. But to me he is a monster. Please, don't ever ask me this again."

He flipped his hood over his head and shut his eyes. He didn't need to see that tears were flooding his mother's eyes, threatening to drown her pupils. He wanted to be invisible. For a moment he thought about the unflattering ways he had heard Rachel talk about Muriel, and he knew he didn't want that for himself. He never wanted his mother to feel he didn't appreciate her. But there was no way he was going to see Darnell. With a care born out of shame, he reached his hand out and gently touched his mother's knee.

When Muriel had called him, he had found her tone curious. She'd actually sounded somewhat cheerful. Since she wanted to see him as soon as possible, he switched schedules with a coworker to make it work. The old lady was waiting for him in the lobby. She looked different. For one, she was wearing a dress, as opposed to her normal khakis and apron. She looked more like she was ready for a night out at Comforti's than a day in the studio. The dress was bright gray and gold. She was wearing makeup and her hair was shiny and kempt, not the ponytail or lopsided bun he'd come to expect. If he didn't know any better, he'd have thought they were going on a date. She immediately took his arm and walked him out of the lobby.

"Come along, young man. I want to share something with you."

They got into the back of an awaiting yellow taxi, and she instructed the driver to go to an unfamiliar address. Her amiable manner disarmed him; he'd only really seen her as grumpy and irascible—both at the restaurant and in the studio. The Muriel sitting beside him in a taxi that reeked of cheap lemon disinfectant appeared to be rosy and anxious. There was a sparkle in her eyes when she spoke to him. For a moment he wondered if she was on something. He couldn't wait to figure out what had changed. As they headed downtown, she explained it to him. She was taking him to a gallery in Soho where several artists she knew and respected were taking part in a show.

When they reached the gallery, he was pleased to see a small but impressive crowd gathered inside the cramped space. They were people like he had never associated with: well dressed, stylish in a funky sort of way. Diverse in ways he didn't expect people with money to be. The hostess was a slender, sexy-looking Japanese woman in a tight black leather dress. She greeted Muriel with a European-style kiss on both cheeks and a hug.

"Megumi, this is Rashid."

"You don't need to tell me his name. I recognized him the minute you got out of the cab."

She took his hand, shook it warmly, and gave him the same European kiss. He was both out of place yet welcomed. He felt other people's eyes on him and couldn't tell if he was being paranoid.

"Can I get either of you a drink?" Megumi asked.

"I'll have a chardonnay. Rashid?"

"Umm, I'll have the same, please."

"Sure, I'll be right back. Muriel, I think you'll find quite the fan base waiting for you over by wall C. If you want, I can meet you there."

"I'm actually going to avoid that area. I want Rashid to take in the other works first."

He walked around the small gallery for about a half hour, just taking in a number of pieces in complete silence. Muriel had insisted to him this was the best way to view art—silent and alone with your reflections. The last piece they arrived at caused the tiniest of earthquakes to rumble within him. It was a nearly two-foot ceramic bust of him, bronze on bronze. Behind it on the wall was the sketch pad drawing she had done of him. He was shirtless, and his jeans were unzipped in the front revealing the top portion of his underwear. The image affected him in a way he never imagined a work could. It was like he was watching a dreamlike version of himself. There was a white card at the bottom of it that read, "SOLD."

"You sold me," he said.

"Something about that sounds terribly tawdry. But yes, you have been sold, and for a handsome amount, I must say. I know the buyer. If it is any consolation, you'll be part of an impressive collection in a lovely home in Darien, Connecticut. Your new owners are a playwright and his entertainment attorney boyfriend. They are both exceptional men."

They toasted to selling out, and then he felt her hand in his. It was an emotional moment for him. When she excused herself to use the restroom, he stood before his statue and took it all in. Within moments Megumi appeared beside him. They both stood in silence for a while.

"So, how does it feel to be immortal?" she broke in.

"I really just don't know what to say. I feel . . . unworthy."

"Everyone says that. Trust me, you're worthy. Muriel doesn't do unworthy."

Outside, the old lady hailed a cab. When it pulled up, she handed him an envelope and signaled for him to take the cab.

"I can't go. I have a stuffy party to attend across the river. There will be enough in this envelope for you to get home. I'll call in a few days to set up our next session."

"Thank you, Muriel. Thank you so much. Say, I never got to ask—how is your daughter?"

"Rachel? She's fine. Same jerk she's always been. Do you have kids?"

"I do not."

"Let me give you a piece of advice—don't. They do nothing but disappoint you. I'm serious. Biggest disappointments of my life have been both of them. Self-centered ingrates to the core."

He watched her walk back inside the gallery, then got in the cab. When he told the driver his address in Brooklyn, the Middle Eastern man winced slightly and took off—no doubt annoyed to have to take a fare over the bridge and into Bed Stuy. He opened the envelope to find five twenty-dollar bills and a check made out to him for $1,200. That was great and all, but the feeling that he couldn't get over was just how special it all felt to him—somehow, in the short span of a few months, both mother and daughter had managed to make him feel different, worthy, beautiful even. He wondered if he had always felt that way but having them in his life had just enhanced his original strength. Kind of the way the Comfortis had taught him that adding cream and sugar to strong Italian coffee brought additional richness to the flavor of the bean.

Ten

He liked being at Stacie's house when her roommate wasn't there. It wasn't like all the other homes in his life, which were all apartments. Her house actually felt like *a home*. She had a yard, a small porch, a garden, two bathrooms, and a living room filled with framed blaxploitation posters, vases with flowers, scented candles, and a full bookshelf. It had a real vibe. There was a teakettle on the stove and a calendar on the wall that depicted a new, cuter puppy every month. It was as close to idyllic as he'd seen. Even Muriel's over-the-top Manhattan apartment didn't feel so comfortable, so perfectly lived-in. He sat on the couch and watched her at her keyboard, a large Casio. She was humming out notes to the music. He had been listening to her songs for over a half hour, and it was starting to bore him, but he wanted to be supportive.

"Okay, last one," she said. Her hair was pulled back into two pigtails, and she wore a baggy one-piece jumpsuit. "This one is, like, her kind of lamenting how she never really had a chance with the Curtis Institute. The working title is 'Black Girls Need Not Apply.'"

Her framed movie poster of Foxy Brown on the wall loomed over her head. In some ways Stacie's mother (his aunt Felicia) reminded him of Pam Grier. Both were sexy badasses who had the weary look in their eyes of women who had seen too much. Aunt Felicia had been a police officer in the Monmouth County section of New Jersey. Rumor had it that she once had a one-night stand with Bruce Springsteen when she was assigned to work his gig as security at the Asbury Park's Stone Pony. Aunt Felicia stubbornly refused to confirm or deny the rumors, citing that "a true lady doesn't kiss and tell." Every time the subject was raised, she would just blush a little, which of course caused many to speculate that Stacie's older sister, Jamira (who was light skinned and played guitar), was the illegitimate daughter of the Boss himself.

> *Y'all shoulda never wasted my time*
> *Coulda saved my stamp, coulda saved the dime*
> *Y'all shoulda told me this was how it was gonna fly*
> *You pretended to make dreams come true, but Black*
>   *girls need not apply . . .*

He was lost in thoughts of Foxy Brown when he realized she had stopped singing.

"You're sick of this shit, ain't you?"

"Sorry, I'm just distracted."

"What are you distracted about?"

"I don't know, Foxy Brown?"

"Niggas ain't got no attention spans, for real." She got up and went over to her purse. She pulled out a joint and lit it. After taking a hit, she passed it to him. "I'll take you back to the train station."

"You don't have to, I can walk."

"No, let me take you. We can have a drink at Cole's on the way."

He puffed on her joint for a few minutes as he sat on the couch. He heard her yell from her bedroom. "Oh my fucking Jesus Christ!"

She came into the room wearing tight blue jeans and a pink lace bra. She had been brushing her hair. "Did you hear?"

"Hear what?"

"Hear the news? They're in talks to release the Central Park Five. Turns out that new evidence is actually valid!"

"What?"

"Just heard it on the news. Yeah, and just like we all said, those police detectives involved pressured some of them into those confessions."

"That wouldn't surprise me."

Cole's Pub was a popular dive with Black and brown folks in the area, and it was packed. A football game played on the television of the smoke-filled bar, and a jukebox played Kool and the Gang. The two of them drank bottled beer and shots of bourbon. He mainly listened, as Stacie had become obsessed with the topic since they left her house.

"Man, when I think about the hatred I felt for those boys—the hatred *they* made us feel—and it was all a lie. It was *all a lie*! And *they* knew it. They needed a scapegoat so that white people could feel safe in their skins. They created a Black monster and we all just played along."

"It's sickening. Those boys lost a dozen years each of their lives."

"A dozen years. Can you imagine? And those assholes had the DNA evidence since last spring. Just unbelievable. I swear to god, it just makes you want to kill whitey, doesn't it? This would have never happened if, say, the details were reversed and it had been a Black woman running in a park in Beverly Hills who was raped, and a bunch of white boys had been spotted in the area. It would never have gone down the same way. There's just no way. And fucking Ray Kelly is still denying any mishandling. God, I hope they sue the pants off this city."

"No amount of money can make up for what they went through."

"True. True. But money is the only way we have to get justice in this society. It's the only thing they hate parting with."

The news swept through his community like a vicious strain of the flu. Anger was palpable everywhere. The exoneration and police misconduct were all people talked about in bodegas, on stoops, in elevators, at bus stops. It was different in Muriel's neighborhood. There, the doormen still nodded at him with a smile. Posters for the Broadway musicals *The Phantom of the Opera*, *Rent*, and *Les Misérables* were in the windows of many phone kiosks, and dog walkers walked ten dogs at once along Central Park.

This time, when he sat for her, it confirmed his suspicion that the old lady was a real Jekyll and Hyde. There would never be any sense of stability where she was concerned. He'd come to know her well enough to be able to tell when she was in another one of her nonproductive moods. A lot of it had to do with how much work she got done in the first fifteen or so minutes of their session. On that afternoon she had barely touched the canvas, just watched him and looked at the floor as he sat there in the punishing sunlight for about twenty minutes.

"I could use some good matzo ball soup. You hungry?"

"I could eat."

Within minutes they were a couple of blocks over, sitting in the back of a delicatessen. She slurped at a huge bowl of soup while he ate a chicken salad sandwich. He watched her often. He was just now starting to realize that he had underestimated how much pain she was in, had been in since he had first met her. He would have to remember to tell Rachel this—that she needed to be kinder to the old lady—if he ever spoke to Rachel again. After a couple of minutes of quiet, she pushed the mostly full bowl away from her and threw her napkin down.

"This is not what I was looking for at all. Quality. Quality, it's a forgotten relic."

"Can we maybe get you something else?"

"No, you can't get me something else. I want what I fucking wanted."

"Sorry."

"'Get you something else.' I tell you, that is part of the problem with your generation. You settle. You settle when you should demand. No one ever got anywhere just settling for things. You think that's okay, do you?"

"I didn't really mean you should settle."

"That's exactly what you implied. *Get you something else.* It's not just a problem with your generation. It's a problem with your people too. You settle when you should be breaking things, tearing things down. You settle and you wait for some God to fix things in the long run. I got news for you, buddy—God is not coming to save you. God is not coming to save any of us. You will choke on that fucking sandwich waiting for God to come save you. Don't get me started. You know, six million Jews looked up to the sky and begged for God to save them while they were being led to the slaughterhouse. Millions of Native Americans looked to the sky and begged for God to save them. Millions of African slaves looked to the sky and begged for God to save them. Millions of Congolese during the Congo War looked to the sky and begged for God to save them. Millions of Tutsi and Hutus looked to the sky and begged for God to save them. Millions of Cambodians fleeing the killing fields looked to the sky and begged for God to save them. Millions in Bangladesh looked to the sky and begged for God to save them. And I'm pretty certain that on 9/11, my husband, along with several thousand others, was looking to the sky and begging for God to save him. And all of these people have one thing in common: God never came. He couldn't be bothered. And you need to get that in your head. God is not coming to save you. God doesn't care whether you win or lose. You have to fend for yourself. If there ever was a God who cared about us, mark my words, he gave up long ago."

Rashid sat for her two more times, and each time, she appeared more grumpy, more easily agitated. He was at a loss for how to bring some levity or comfort to their sessions. He imagined this must be what it was like to watch a marriage dissolve. The day before Thanksgiving, as he was getting dressed in Muriel's bathroom after posing for nearly two hours, he heard Muriel knock on the door.

"Hey, listen, see yourself out. I have to run an emergency errand for a friend. I left you a card on the kitchen table."

When he emerged from the bathroom, he zipped up his hefty down coat and went straight for her kitchen. It felt awkward to be in her place alone, yet there was also something flattering about her feeling comfortable enough to have him there. He went to the table where there was a white envelope with his name on it, propped up against a box of vanilla wafers.

He grabbed the envelope and opened it. He sat by the window and read the card after pocketing the three hundred-dollar bills that were inside.

Dear Rashid, I detest goodbyes, and because I am such a coward, I chose to do it this way. Our time has come to an end. I have drawn all of the inspiration that I can from you, and it is time for me to move on and find a new muse. This will be our last session. It is possible I will stop into Comforti's from time to time, but most likely not until the spring when it gets warmer. May I give you a few words of advice on the way out? Take it or leave it. You are way too smart and thoughtful to be a waiter much longer. You have much to offer, and I would suggest you consider going to school and getting a degree in something, anything. Do you like kids? You might make a great teacher. Anyway, whatever path you choose, I wish you well. You have been a wonderful source, and I hope I wasn't too terrible to you. You are an admirable human being. With Appreciation, M.

He read the card about three times before he folded it up and placed it in his back pocket. He thought to leave, but another stronger sentiment gripped him. He darted to Muriel's bedroom to a spot he knew on her dresser. There were several framed pictures of Muriel and her husband, the entire family, solo pictures of each grandchild, and a few of her children there. Rashid had always been fond of one picture of Rachel that sat tucked into the upper corner of the mirror. It was of a teenaged Rachel standing in front of a brown horse on a ranch. She was wearing a plaid skirt, a blue blouse, and she had a yellow rose in her hair. She didn't appear to know the picture was being taken, because she was looking away at something over her shoulder. She held a flute. He snatched the picture out of its place, and after a few seconds of reflection, he shoved it into his back pocket and walked out of the apartment for what he assumed would be the last time.

Eleven

The holiday season was always a mixed bag for Rashid and his mother. Their shared memories of his childhood, both in their tiny apartment and in his aunt Cecily's roomier, more welcoming house on Staten Island. There were fake trees that had dangerously sharp cones and smelled like artificial pine. There were stockings and eggnog and all the silly stuff, but it never really added up to holiday cheer. In order to have a truly merry time around the holidays, all television and movies informed Rashid that there was one dire, necessary component: a strong family unit. This was where most people he knew failed and failed hard. His situation was no exception. One holiday season, his father broke into their apartment and stole a television set. Another time, Aunt Merna got so drunk at the Thanksgiving table that she wound up getting into a fight with his mother about an ancient sibling grievance around a boy they'd both had a crush on at Sunday school. In the end, Aunt Cecily wound up kicking them all out into the frigid cold around midnight.

Of all the family dysfunction that took place around the holidays, there was one memory that seared itself into his brain. He had just started junior high school when he and Darnell went out on a Christmas Eve, and Darnell decided it would be a perfect time to steal a CD player from an electronics shop on Fulton Street. Darnell had it all planned out, and as usual, even though Rashid didn't feel comfortable about it, he went along because Darnell, the older brother, was convincing and intimidating.

"Don't be a punk-ass pussy like those other guys you hang with," was Darnell's consistent line of reassurance.

On this night, the plan was simple—they would walk into the store together and immediately split up. He would pepper the store manager, a big dude from New Delhi, with a series of questions about a VCR, distracting the man, while Darnell, already positioned in the back, stuffed as many portable CD players as he could under his sheepskin coat. Again, a real simple plan. "Even an idiot couldn't fuck this up," was how Darnell put it to him.

"The best laid schemes of mice and men," was the reference Marlon would make every time they discussed it, which was just about every Christmas Eve.

He had walked up to the manager at his counter roughly thirty seconds after they entered. Rashid pointed to a couple of VCRs behind the man and started asking about various features and wondering about recording speeds. The man had been eating a meaty gyro and began answering him with a full mouth. It took barely two minutes of this charade before someone started shouting loudly from the back of the store and Darnell went racing by Rashid with a much younger, much skinnier Indian man chasing after him. The man behind the counter moved fast. He had shoved his gyro aside, grabbed a bat from behind the counter, and run to the front doorway, thus blocking any entry or exit before Rashid even had time to react.

Rashid froze for a few seconds and then looked around for a rear exit. Before he could make out any possible escape, the younger Indian man was back, clutching a bleeding hand. Later Rashid would learn that the man had caught up to Darnell, who'd met him with a swinging switchblade as the clerk tried to grab him by his jacket collar. Rashid had seen Darnell flexing with his switchblade periodically at home in front of the mirror, but he never dreamed he would actually ever use it. The two men from the store talked in front of the door, and their attention went straight to him. He knew that they knew, and he wanted very much to run, but there was nowhere to go.

The bigger man threw him to the ground and stepped on his wrist to hold him in place, and the younger one called the police while bandaging his blood-dripping hand. Rashid's wrist and whole arm were in pain, and he watched, frightened, as the man pointed a beefy finger at him and said in a thick native accent: "You think we don't know what you stupid monkeys are up to? You think we come here as fucking morons? You wait—you will be spending Christmas in jail, you fucking monkey!"

The rest of the night went very quickly. Two police officers came and took everyone's statements (he stuck to the story that he barely knew Darnell, had bumped into him as they entered the store), and eventually his mother was called and told she had to come to the store to pick him up before the police would let him go. There were heated words between his mother and the police, and especially vile words for the manager once she discovered that he had been physically aggressive with her son. Rashid could count on one hand the times that he had ever seen his mother outraged, and each instance had to do with her perception that someone had behaved inappropriately towards one of her children.

When all was over, the police had to let him go. They didn't have any evidence tying him to Darnell (who had managed to get three CD players under his wing before making a break for it). As Rashid and his mother walked out of the store, the manager followed them with his bat and yelled: "Make sure you know, I see you in here ever again, I bash your fucking brains in."

His mother lit into him on the way home. She had already seen Darnell and knew that something bad had gone down, and she made it clear that she expected more out of him than she did his brother. Thank goodness for him he had gotten to that age that most mothers despise—when their child is too old and has grown too big to be beaten with a belt. He got the verbal equivalent of a good lashing for the rest of the night, and when Darnell returned home from his girlfriend's place the next morning with an Egg McMuffin and a soda, he simply laughed at him.

"Nigga, you need to learn to run faster. God gave you them skinny-ass legs for a reason!"

Worst of all, Darnell had already sold the CD players. It had all been for naught; Rashid had gotten nothing in return. Whenever people asked him about his relationship with his brother, the CD player incident was one of a dozen reflections that he could fall back on to justify his feelings.

Now that he was an adult, the holidays had gotten a little easier. Rashid came to the great discovery that you don't necessarily have to depend on your family for happiness at holiday time, or at any time, for that matter. He realized family was a concept that had great limitations. Yes, family was blood, and blood was thicker than water. But, as the years went on, he learned a valuable lesson that he would carry with him forever: just because someone is family does not mean you have to like them. Family can hurt you in the same ways, if not worse, than the stranger on the street. Darnell was his greatest example. And as he had witnessed with Rachel and Muriel, this concept flowed across all culture lines. Rachel couldn't stand her mother. Her mother, in turn, did not exhibit affection for either of her children. In fact, if you were fortunate enough to have people you liked in your life, you could *create* your own family. Family was whom *you* chose, and it could be comprised of those who made you feel most loved and appreciated. Ever since he had begun working for the Comfortis, he had been invited into their universe with open arms, and without design or any conscious awareness of it, *they* became part of his chosen family. When he first decided to spend Christmas with the Comfortis, his mother had been confused and acted hurt. It had never occurred to him that being away from both her sons during Christmas would be a source of anguish for her. But she spent the holidays with her sister, surrounded by family. She got used to the idea eventually, or at least she stopped bringing it up.

This Christmas he felt especially grateful to be with the Comfortis. After closing the restaurant on Christmas Eve, Rashid always spent the night at Antony and Lucia Comforti's home in Mott Haven, sharing a bedroom with the youngest son, Carlo, who lived in Minneapolis. First thing in the morning, Antony and his cousins went ice-skating in Saint Mary's Park, followed by hot chocolate and doughnuts at Satriani's. In the afternoon, Rashid and Antony went shopping with Antony's son for all the alcohol they planned to consume throughout the day.

In the early evening, Antony and Aunt Gina sang Christmas duets on a rented karaoke machine. After dinner, they all sat around, drank, smoked cigars, and played poker well into the night while *It's a Wonderful Life* played in the background. In the midst of her ferocious effort to clean up after everyone, Lucia would walk by with a fresh new glass of wine for him. He liked the way the scent of garlic and baking powder clung to her as she placed the full glass down beside his chair, kissed his forehead, and walked away with the empty glass. Occasionally, Aunt Gina would slip him an extra piece of white chocolate as he played cards with whomever was still awake and not too drunk. Rashid would spend that night there as well, then head to Comforti's with Antony and Lucia to open the next day. At some point in the afternoon, he would make a discovery: a crisp one-hundred-dollar bill folded neatly in his coat pocket, compliments of Uncle Rudy, who gave that gift "to all of my children."

If he spent every holiday season with the Comfortis for the rest of his life, it would have been just fine with him. They filled a void deep within him.

At Stacie's New Year's Eve party, he was not in the mood for socializing, and he retreated to her bedroom at around ten p.m. He closed the door and walked over to her record player, which sat on a table beside a typewriter. He flipped through her crate of albums on the floor beside her bed and carried one over to the player, removing the Prince album that she'd been playing. He placed the vinyl gently on the turntable and moved the needle to a select spot. He then lit a cigarette and listened as "Once in a Blue Moon" filled the room. He smiled, momentarily transported back to a simpler time. The spell was interrupted when the bedroom door opened and Kenya walked in. He looked up at her, frustrated to be back in reality.

"What are you doing?" she asked, standing a foot away.

He had first met Kenya Ingram at a reading that a local author gave at Stacie's bookstore. It had been planned, basically a blind date organized by his cousin. She was the sister who could cook that Stacie had mentioned. His first impression was that Kenya was smart, easy on the eyes, and a little on the young side, she'd just turned drinking age. But he was more than willing, desperate to try to heal the still-raw scars left by Rachel.

After the reading, a small group went out to a local bar, and there he sat by Kenya, and the two talked for hours. She was from a small family outside Detroit and grew up a practicing Jehovah's Witness. But she'd abandoned the religion, ostracizing her from her parents, after dropping out of a small community college and moving to New York with a fellow student she had fallen in love with. The relationship had only lasted two months, but she was extremely grateful to leave behind all she had known and "reset her life," as she put it. She attended a culinary school in Manhattan a few nights a week.

On their first date they went to an art exhibit in Fort Greene Park. Their conversation was fluid and easy, but he also was annoyed by the number of times she used "like" in her sentences, and he couldn't help but judge the loudness of her tone. He wanted to remind her that he was right next to her and not hard of hearing.

She had a penchant for tight skirts and with damn good reason. She had lanky, toned swimmer's arms, magnificent hips, and what Marlon commonly referred to as "grand Aretha Franklin" booty. And Kenya was a phenomenal dancer. Their second date was at a club in the Bronx, where she pressed up tightly against him on the dance floor. She was a bonified catch, and he knew many guys who would step on their grandmothers' necks to take her home at night. But it wasn't until after her roommates went to sleep and they entered her tiny bedroom in Canarsie that he realized it was actually too soon for any type of relationship.

As he kissed her shoulder, he could not help but remember how Rachel's shoulder had smelled their first night. Although it got easier and more enjoyable each time Rashid returned to Kenya's bedroom, he was sure that their relationship would never truly be right. For reasons he wasn't quite ready to understand, he would never genuinely love Kenya. He just didn't know how to articulate it. Now, with the orchestra closing out on "Once in a Blue Moon," he wanted to hear the song once more. He longed for the solitude he had found in the room moments earlier.

"I just wanted some quiet time."

"Quiet time? You feeling okay?"

"I feel fine. Sometimes a crowd can feel suffocating, you know?"

He watched her smooth face twist into a curious smile. She was wearing huge circular glasses that highlighted her chestnut eyes. Her dreadlocks silhouetted her neck and shoulders. She licked at her full brown lips and crossed her arms. He knew that she didn't feel fully appreciated by him. They had discussed it a couple of times already—how he always seemed to hold her at a distance.

"Is the crowd suffocating, Rashid, or am I?"

When he didn't answer right away, she closed the door behind her and left him alone with his memories, the place where he most wanted to be. He didn't follow.

Twelve

It was that perfect time of the day at Comforti's when the afternoon crowd thinned out and there were two or three patrons in the place. There was a decent ninety minutes to two hours before the dinner crowd would start, and he could just sit with himself. He and Stacie had made a pledge to each other for Black History Month: they would each read at least three books by African American writers over the twenty-eight days of February. He had been planning to finally read *Anna Karenina*, which he had recently gotten from the library, but Stacie had said, "Fuck that Russian soap opera shit," and convinced him to join her challenge.

He sat at the bar with his first selection, a collection of James Baldwin essays he had found at Stacie's store. A cigarette that he didn't plan to smoke sat over his ear—he had promised Lucia that with the new year he would quit smoking, until April at the least. The respite periodically drove him crazy, but he was saving a lot of money.

He was halfway through the book, and although he had heard of the man, he had no idea he would come to feel so strongly about him. He had developed a great admiration for Mr. Baldwin. He and Kenya had recently gone to see a production of his play, *Blues for Mister Charlie*, at a small theatre in Williamsburg, and he told himself that if someday he could have half the intellectual capacity of Baldwin, he would do okay for himself in life. The question he now pondered was:

How does one become an intellectual? What is that process like? When he had posed the question to Marlon a few days ago, his friend's response was, as always, succinct: "Nigga, you sure don't get to be no intellectual waitin' tables."

"Gotta pay rent too, don't I?"

"You asked the question, not me."

Rashid opened the book and thumbed through it. Baldwin had so many things to say to him about his own current situation, and it amazed him to realize the man had written all of it decades ago, before Rashid or his mother had been born.

Antony, who had been cleaning the bar with a rag and a bottle of disinfectant, was about to pass him a snifter of cognac to enjoy, but he pulled it back.

"Oops, not now," Antony told him. "Table four."

A customer had just entered, and Rashid raised his head from his book, resenting the interruption. The sight of a familiar silhouette left him breathless. His legs were shakier than normal as he made his way over to the table where Rachel sat perusing the menu. He pulled out his pad.

"I was wondering how long it took to get service in this place," she said with a smile that couldn't mask her fear.

"Rachel."

"Please forgive me for coming here, please. I had to."

"It's okay. What can I get you?"

"Rashid, there's a lot I have to explain to you."

"You don't have to explain anything to me."

He had never experienced a tremor in his life, but it felt to him like this was what that must feel like—to not be secure with the ground underneath you.

"I do, actually. I really do. There's a bar two blocks down on Fordham Road, Padrinos. Will you meet me there after your shift?"

"It isn't a good idea, Rachel."

"Please. Please. If I have to, I'll beg you."

He looked around. Antony and another waitress at the bar were watching them.

"I came here to see you. Got in my car and drove four hours. I haven't been able to stop thinking about you for weeks, months really."

Every feature about her was the same, but there was a more pronounced look of exhaustion around her eyes. He could see her lower lip trembling. He wanted to reach out and touch her, ease whatever she was feeling. It was then that he knew he never really had a choice.

Padrinos was dark and smelled like stale beer and burnt popcorn. It was the kind of place that bearded old grandfathers and uncles from the neighborhood were proud to call their oasis. A Led Zeppelin song played on the jukebox. He found her sitting at the end of the bar with a glass of red wine. The saddest part of her was that she didn't appear out of place there. She was looking in the direction of two Puerto Rican guys playing pool, but he could tell she wasn't actually involved in the game itself. Her thoughts were elsewhere. As he approached, the grin that formed on her face seemed forced. He took a seat beside her, unzipping his coat.

"Thank you for coming."

"You don't have to thank me."

"No, I do. I'm sure there are other places you'd rather be right now."

He signaled for the bartender and ordered a bourbon with a beer back. He went to light a cigarette from a freshly purchased pack, before remembering his promise to Lucia. He cursed under his breath as he blew out the match.

"Secondhand smoke is a killer," he heard her say, uncomfortably. There was a drawn-out silence between them that stretched in front of him like a moat. She kept a journal, she told him. Always had. Her husband had discovered her journal. He always knew where it was. He had read everything. Pages and pages had been about Rashid. About her and him. About her passion for him. There were poems addressed to him, small stanzas. The journal had caused her husband to have an emotional breakdown. He began weeping uncontrollably and often, begging her for a second chance. He promised her he could change. He threatened to kill himself. She promised him she would agree to go to counseling. She promised her husband she would end the affair. That promise, she realized now, was a mistake.

They went to counseling, several sessions. Her heart wasn't in it. Her husband kept saying things that weren't true. He kept blaming her for not being there emotionally. She realized she hated the sound of her husband's voice. Hated his hands. Hated his smell. He didn't change.

She drank. She got into a car accident. She nearly hit a teenager on a bicycle. She was arrested for driving under the influence. She could not continue that way. She needed to see Rashid again. She had always thought of him. She had started divorce proceedings. She was living in a one-bedroom apartment miles from her children. She knew she had to see Rashid, if only to explain. She had never wanted to hurt him. She had never expected it to get to where it had gotten. He put his hand up to stop her.

"You don't owe me any apology. I'm a grown man. I knew what I was getting into. You don't have to do this. But thank you, though, for reaching out."

"It's more than just reaching out."

"Well whatever it is, thank you. I appreciate it. I should get going."

"It appalls you to be around me."

"It doesn't appall me."

"You despise me. I knew you would."

"I don't despise you."

"You've barely been able to look me in the eye for ten seconds straight since I first walked into Comforti's."

"What do you want, Rachel, huh? You just up and disappeared like I was some diseased leper. Do you know how that felt?"

"In some ridiculous way I thought I was doing what was best for you."

"As if you know what's best for me."

"It was unreasonable to an extent."

"Unreasonable. That's funny."

"Not a day went by when—"

"Spare me, okay? Please do me that favor and just spare me?"

They sat in silence for minutes, and the whole time, he kept thinking about the day she had given him his flute. How special and beloved that act had made him feel. Led Zeppelin turned into Marvin Gaye, which turned into Donna Summer. He wanted to flee but his legs would not listen to his brain.

"What kind of person just leaves like that? Leaves without a word and doesn't look back? What kind of person rips another person open and just leaves them there to bleed all over the floor?"

"I was confused, Rashid."

"*You* were confused? Priceless. Well, in case you were wondering, I'm okay. I'm better now. I'm fully recovered, and I am stronger for it. It took a while, but I got there."

"I knew you would be. You may be the strongest person I know."

"There is no maybe about it. I am the strongest person you know. Goodbye, Rachel."

He placed a ten-dollar bill on the bar and walked out into the freezing night. He'd gotten as far as the corner when she rushed up beside him. She had left her coat inside.

"Rashid, please. I fucked up. I know it. It's why I'm here. Please."

"What do you want, Rachel? What do you want from me?"

"I want you to forgive me."

"You're forgiven," he said, trying hard to mean it.

"Thank you."

He headed up the stairs of the subway station, his legs taking him from where his heart wanted to be.

"Don't you want anything from me?" he heard her yell into the cold air.

Thirteen

And just like that, Rashid was drowning in his sleep again. He woke up to the image of Rachel alone at that decrepit bar. He should never have left her there. He should have at least gotten her into a taxi. She was an adult; he was not responsible for her. In the shower, he cursed himself for not getting her into a taxi. He called her from his bedroom. He was relieved to hear her voice.

"I just wanted to make sure you got home okay."

"I did, thank you. I'm staying at my mother's. It's sweet of you to check in on me."

"I felt bad. I should have gotten you in a cab last night."

"I'm so sorry, Rashid, for everything."

"Just take care of yourself, Rachel."

"Do you still play your flute?"

He hung up.

During count the rats, he made out six of the critters roaming the tracks before his train roared in. Just then he remembered that Kenya had called him three times over the night, leaving him two voice mails. The sad truth that he hadn't even thought about her all morning told him something that he wasn't ready to acknowledge. He called her as he emerged from the subway.

"What the fuck, Rashid?"

"I'm sorry. I got really distracted last night."

"Obviously. You still want to go tonight, or what?"

"Go where?"

Her sigh on the other end jogged his memory; she had gotten them tickets to an all-Black production of *Hamlet* at BAM tonight. The actor playing Hamlet was some celebrity from a television show he'd never heard of.

"Oh shit, *Hamlet*! That's right. Yeah, no, we good. What time should I be there?"

"You don't have to go, Rashid. I have two friends who couldn't get tickets who would kill each other to go with me."

"Kenya, come on . . ."

He sat on a bench at a nearby bus stop and closed his eyes. He could envision the disappointed look on Kenya's face clearly. He had seen it several times before.

"Don't you 'Come on' me, Rashid, you don't have to go. I swear, lately it feels like I have to force-feed you to get you to do something with me."

"Don't be like that, Kenya. I'm looking forward to this. I'm just . . . distracted lately."

"What else is new?"

He slipped into Comforti's through the back-alley entrance and went straight downstairs to his locker in the basement. He smoked a cigarette as he changed into his black button-down. Kelli, the early-shift opener, came up beside him as he was picking out his Afro in the mirror. They had never had much to say to each other. She was the kind of woman who believed every man was a privileged species capable of rape and murder at the drop of a dime. Her head was shaved practically bald, and she was a hardcore bodybuilder. God help any man who attempted to get in her pants. Her girlfriend was a Brazilian law student. He wondered what they were like alone. She tapped his shoulder with an envelope.

"Hey, Tupac. Looks like you have a secret admirer."

He looked at the envelope. It was small and light, with his name written in a dark marker across the front of it.

"Where did you get this?"

"Chick walked in as soon as we opened, asked if you'd be on today, and handed it to me. Gave me ten dollars to see to it that it was personally delivered to you. I didn't know you rolled with such an esteemed crowd."

He barely heard her response, he was so focused on the penmanship of his name. The writer had taken care with the letters, from *R* to *D*.

"Thank you," he said to her reflection in the mirror.

"Sure thing. Heads up, we're out of tiramisu."

When he was all alone, he opened the envelope. There were two neatly folded pages inside, and Rachel's perfume was on each page. First, he read a small note attached that was on yellow paper, different from the other pages.

Dearest Rashid,

I have wanted to share this with you for some time but haven't felt comfortable doing so until now. I guess I have nothing to lose with you at this point. I'm sure you've lost all respect for me, and I honestly don't blame you. I may deserve that. I just wanted to give you a glimpse into how you touched me. This is just one journal entry from a very special day for me last summer.

He read the other pages, ripped from a book.

Yesterday I gave him my first flute, the one Daddy had gotten me when I was a junior at Churchill. I've wanted him to have it since the first time we were together, and it just felt right to give it now. He's come to have an appreciation for classical music in our short time together, and it is so powerful to know that our relationship has changed him in any small way. To know that I have touched him, burrowed into him, shaped him. I could see that he was moved by it, and when he put it to his lips, I just wanted to cry. For me, this is what love is truly about. It is about touching and being touched. It is about appreciating and being appreciated. It is about mattering in someone else's life. I haven't mattered in Michael's life for years now. And, truth be told, he hasn't really mattered in mine. We live together. We are parents of children, but we are more like roommates in a sense. Roommates with parenting duties. We are laborers. We have a responsibility to each other that is all tied to raising healthy children. There is nothing else. He will never grow with me. I will never grow with him. I'm not sure we ever knew passion. We knew lust. We knew desire. With Rashid, it is night and day.

The first time I ever kissed Rashid on the neck, I felt his body shiver. I had not known that I could elicit that response in a man. It excited me. And my excitement in turn excited him. It was a lovely circle. He shares things with me. He is not afraid to be vulnerable with me. When he told me the terrible story about his brother, I saw a shadow envelop his entire being. I wanted to embrace him, but I fear it will not be enough. He has known a type of pain that I could never know. He was raised in cracked brick and broken glass, in apartment buildings in a world I will never know and could only imagine. We are absolutely different, and that will be our inevitable downfall. But I want to live in the now, and for now I want him in my life. I want him for as long as

I can have him. I feel like I deserve him, and he deserves me. It is probably selfish of me, but I really don't care at this point. I want all of it. I always want to feel how I feel when he is under me, with him clutching my breasts like a drowning man grasping for the surface of the ocean. I want to give way to the music. He is my composition.

He read the pages over and over. But one line in particular reverberated in him like a church bell in a tunnel: *Clutching my breasts like a drowning man grasping for the surface of the ocean.*

With a sigh, he tucked the pages gently back into the envelope. He leaned against the locker and looked at his face in the mirror. It wasn't clear to him just who he saw reflected back. Before he fully realized what he was doing, his phone was in his palm. She answered on the first ring. Muriel was out of town. Her work was being shown at a gallery on the West Coast. They could just talk like adults. She would buy the blueberry muffins he liked so much. They could just talk. It was important to see him.

He lied to the day manager—told him he felt feverish, which wasn't a complete lie. It took him forty minutes to get to Muriel's apartment. The doorman told him it was good to see him again. Called him "sir." It took him seconds to remove the robe from her shoulders, to see the white skin underneath it, glowing like an exposed bone. He knelt to kiss her smooth belly. Without reservation, he returned to the childhood lake he had once drowned in.

Dinner was Vivaldi and delivered Chinese food. It was peculiar to sit at Muriel's table, eating on her china, after the incendiary hours in her bed, but he could think of no place he'd rather be. And yet, he was due at a bar in Brooklyn in an hour. As he showered, she stood in the door of the bathroom in her robe and nibbled on snow peas.

"Any chance you can get back here tonight?"

"I don't know. We're supposed to go to an after-party."

"What's she like, your Kenya?"

"She's nice. Thoughtful. Smart."

"Is she pretty? I bet she's lovely."

"She is pretty."

She was still nibbling on snow peas and staring out the window when he entered the living room fully dressed. He picked up his backpack.

"Isn't it funny how the tables turn? Now it's you leaving to return to your partner."

"I wouldn't necessarily call her my partner. We've been dating."

"You sleep with her."

"Yes."

The aggression of her next act caught him unaware and made him slightly dizzy. She was grasping at him, both angry and desperate.

"I don't want her hands on you. I don't want her lips on you."

"You don't have the—"

"You're mine, Rashid! You're mine!"

"Rachel, I can't . . ."

"I know, I know. Just go." Her grip loosened. "When do you think you can come back?"

"Tomorrow night? After my shift ends."

"I'll look forward to that. I know I have no right to feel this way, Rashid. I have no right to keep you from someone who is probably better for you than I am."

"Don't say any more, please. I'll call you in the morning."

"Call me tonight!"

He was relieved to see Stacie with the group of friends Kenya had organized to meet at the bar. He pulled up a chair and joined Kenya at the head of the table. She barely made eye contact with him after saying

"Hi" quickly and continuing her conversation with a group of girl-friends. He made his way to the bar and ordered a beer.

The play was intriguing, but what really stood out to him was that Kenya did not so much as hold his hand or say twenty words to him during the entire first act. At intermission he watched her get up, excuse herself to use the restroom, and walk off. He sat alone for a while. Eventually Stacie came up beside him.

"So, what do you think?" she asked.

"It's good. I've never really been a Shakespeare guy, but this is good. You?"

"I find Ophelia a bit annoying, but it's okay. Listen, um, are you okay?"

"Yeah, I'm fine. Why? Do I not look it?"

"No, it's just, I wanted to check in. You know if you ever need someone to talk to, I'm here."

Her tone was curious. After the show, he found out what she was actually getting at. Kenya's friend had driven a large station wagon to the show, and the plan was for a group of them to drive over to the after-party together, but Kenya asked him to take a walk with her. It was a bitterly cold night, but he agreed and they walked slowly.

"Listen," she said. "I don't want to draw this out or anything. That isn't my style. I'm a pretty perceptive girl, Rashid. I can read people pretty well. I know when a brother's heart isn't in it, and yours ain't in it." He just nodded and looked down. "I don't know what exactly is going on with you, but you know—we aren't clicking here. You never initiate spending time with me, and when we do spend time together, I get the feeling you'd rather be elsewhere. If I'm wrong, feel free to disagree with me."

She went on like that for a few minutes and he simply nodded and listened, nodded and listened. In the end, she wished him well and told him that she hoped he found what he was looking for someday. In an hour, he was back in Muriel's bed, Rachel sweating.

Fourteen

"Wait. *She* broke up with *you*?" Marlon was beside himself. They were at the local pizzeria, eating a pie with sausage and splitting a plate of garlic knots. "That shit don't make no sense."

"She was right. She deserves someone who is gonna be more present. Someone who is gonna worship her for the queen she is."

"Didn't you say the sex was great?"

"It's not just about that, Marlon."

"Don't get all Dr. Ruth on me, okay? I know a thing or two in this area. How come you couldn't worship her? She got some kind of defect?"

"No, she don't got some kind of defect. If anything, it's me with the defect."

"Elaborate."

He bit his lip and shoved a piece of sausage in his mouth. He didn't want to say it, but he had to tell someone, and Marlon was his most reliable friend.

"Rachel reached back out to me."

"Rachel? Aw, shit. You can't be serious."

"She stopped by Comforti's to see me."

"Stopped by Comforti's? Oh shit, nigga, you fucking her again, ain't you? Oh shit, yeah you are. I could tell by your demeanor. Tell me you ain't."

He looked down and out the pizzeria window at a light snow that was beginning to fall.

"Niggas are something, boy. Three hundred years ago they brought us all over here on these huge-ass ships and they told us—'Pick this fucking cotton! Pick it 'til you bleed! Pick it all day and all night! Oh, by the way, you can fuck your own women—hell, have twenty kids if you want. But whatever you do—do not put your hands on these white women over here! Don't even think it!' We listened to half of what they said. It's like it was too much for us, the whole forbidden-fruit shit. We was Eve and they was the apple. Don't ever demand a person don't do something. They gonna wanna do it. Psychology 101."

"What makes you so sure I've started fucking her again?"

"What? Nigga, this don't take Columbo to figure out. Your ass is weak, and she had you eating out of her hand the first time. Got you listening to Beethoven and shit. You gonna deny it now?"

He bit harder into his slice of pizza, resentful he ever brought it up.

"That's what I thought. Shit is more obvious than a horoscope. What you gonna tell me next, Soylent Green is people?"

He was reading from his James Baldwin book on the subway. A distinguished older Black man in a business suit sat across from him. He hadn't noticed the man watching him. The man spoke up with a baritone, commanding voice.

"He was one of our greatest minds."

"Sir?"

"Baldwin. He was one of our greatest minds. Was closely aligned with some of our greatest thinkers: Malcolm X, Martin, Lorraine Hansberry. But he hated Richard Wright. Hated him with a fury. What does that tell you? That two of our greatest literary heavyweights couldn't see eye to eye on the subject of Blackness?"

"Honestly, sir, I don't know what it tells me."

"Well I'll tell you then—it tells you that we are fucked. Black can't even appreciate Black. We who need each other most can't even have our own backs. Each generation perpetually doomed to eat our own."

He smiled at the man and made a note to learn more about Richard Wright.

The restaurant Rachel chose was a Japanese one in the Financial District. He hated sushi, but it was one of her favorites. He poked at tender pieces of chicken karaage, grateful to see her. Muriel was returning tomorrow afternoon, and this was going to be their last night together for a couple of weeks. She surprised him with the news that she had quit the Boston Philharmonic shortly after her DUI conviction. She was focused on getting a teaching job at a university. She had many applications in, including at Juilliard.

"How would that look if you got a job here?"

"Very good question. I would probably move in with my brother for a while until I could get my own place."

"Not your mom?"

"Oh, no. Oh, hell no. One of us would kill the other."

When the waiter came by, Rachel ordered a third glass of wine. It struck him as peculiar that despite her DUI, she still drank rather heavily.

"What would happen with your kids, do you think?"

"Oh, we'd split the time, I imagine, depending on time of year, schooling needs. Honestly, I'm still trying to figure all of that out. How are your nannying skills?"

He couldn't tell if she was joking. That night, they took a bath together with candlelight and Mozart. The back of her head rested in the center of his chest.

"Maybe next time I'll let you pick the music," she said. "What would you choose?"

"I'm thinking something precious and harmonic, like Wu-Tang Clan."

"Hmm. Maybe I'll continue to pick."

"Oh, come on. Surely your horizons can be expanded too."

"I suppose. But can't we start out with something lighter? I hear Run-DMC are nice fellows."

"Man, I am truly in love with a white girl."

"And don't you forget it."

To celebrate the sixth anniversary of the restaurant, Lucia and Antony gave every employee a bottle of chianti and a commemorative wineglass. He brought both with him to Stacie's bookstore, and as she closed up shop, they drank together. She had news to celebrate: her musical on the life of Nina Simone had taken second place in a nationwide competition run by a theatre company in Louisiana. She showed him the $500 check she'd recently received, which she planned to copy and frame.

He toasted her. "Here's to the great work: Ms. Simone, Brown Baby."

"The first of many more," she responded. They drank half the bottle there as they talked about her recent date with a graduate student at the University of Rhode Island. They had met on an Amtrak train, and though she found him appealing and bright, she had a hard time getting over the fact that he had voted for George W. Bush in the last presidential election. To Stacie, this was one of the ultimate sins a Black person could commit. "Few things are more hideous in this country than the Republican Negro."

He felt a strong urge to tell Stacie about Rachel; he could really use the advice of someone who wasn't Marlon. But he knew it wouldn't go over well, and he feared her judgment. He knew more than anything that her first question would simply be "Why her?" He had no way to articulate any of it. And deep down he didn't want to explain it to anybody. He only knew that with Rachel, he felt needed, desired, listened to, and appreciated. Seeing her broke up the monotony of his routine life. In a myriad of ways, he found release within her.

They made plans to head to a nearby bar. He watched her from the sidewalk as she locked up and keyed in the code for the alarm.

"Hey, do you have any idea what work took first place?"

"Of course I do. It was exactly what you'd expect." They walked down the busy block, which was bustling with people enjoying the evening spring air. "I lost to a one-woman show about Anne Frank. A person of color will never stand a chance against anything Holocaust related. E-V-E-R!"

"Oh, come, come now. That isn't fair."

"You're telling me it isn't fair."

"No, I mean, come on. Isn't it possible that that one-woman show was just maybe a little better than yours?"

"I suppose it's possible. I mean anything is possible. But let's be real here. It is most likely the case that eighty to eighty-five percent of the people on the selection committee were Jewish. If you're a Jew, whose story are you more interested in—a feisty, stubborn Black woman who railed against racial injustice and inequality, or a little Jewish girl who we've all had to learn about since junior high school?"

"I think that's a very cynical viewpoint there, cuz."

"I see. I think it's really interesting that you even have an opinion on this."

"What do you mean?"

"I mean, cuz, that you of all people wouldn't really know much about racism in this industry, or any number of industries, for that matter, because you never put yourself out there. You're not on the front lines of anything. Your utter lack of ambition kind of puts you in this comfortable place where you never really have to challenge anything. You work in a profession in which tips play a crucial role, and as a result, you are pretty willing to be treated any way as long as you don't ruffle any feathers."

They were at a streetlight now, and although the light was green, he refused to move forward. "Did you really just say I haven't experienced racism?"

"No, that is not what I said. What I said was, unlike me, or my mother, or your mother, or Kenya, you don't live in a place where you are confronted with the struggle of trying to move forward every day, *every day*, in a world with its heart set on keeping you in your place. You don't put yourself out there for that kind of struggle. You don't look the beast straight in the eyes like we do. You have your little Italian mom and pop over there in the Bronx, who will be happy to have you stay on as a waiter with no health insurance and no retirement plan for the rest of your life, and you seem pretty content to ride that out. Am I wrong? Please correct me if I'm wrong here, cuz."

"I think you are underestimating me."

"Am I?"

"Yeah, you are. And I get it. You are angry. You think you should have come in first. You always think you should come in first. Always have, ever since we were kids. I get it. You're angry. You always think the Man is denying you something. It's convenient for you."

"Convenient? Do you even know what convenient means?"

"Don't get all testy with me, Stacie. I'm just saying you never think it's about you. It's always someone else done you wrong. And it concerns me because you just seem angry a lot. Almost all the time."

"I hear that. I hear what you are saying. And I guess the only response I have to that is yeah, you're damn right I'm angry. Fuck yeah, I'm angry. Your blues ain't like mine, Shid. And the one question I would have for you is why aren't you angry too? Huh? You've been held back by the system. Where is your anger, Negro?"

After this conversation, whenever he scooped up his tips at Comforti's, he felt a tinge of shame. He began to question his purpose. He started to ask himself things that troubled him. *What are you doing with your life? What is your purpose in all of this?* He called Rachel first chance he had on his lunch break. He didn't share his entire conversation with Stacie, just the portion where she had called him unambitious.

"I would say that your cousin is being a little harsh, but that is what people sometimes do when they love you. They don't pull punches."

"Do you think I lack ambition as well?"

"Everybody has their own clock. Do I think you want to be a waiter forever? No."

"It's not like I have a lot of opportunity, you know? I'm playing the hand I was dealt."

"Are you, though? Your cousin might say she was dealt the same hand, maybe even a worse one."

"Yeah, right. Minus the drug-addicted father and gang-involved, murderous brother."

"I'm just saying, at some point you have to decide, look at yourself in the mirror. If you are happy where you are, then that should be enough. I ask you—are you happy where you are?"

He didn't know how to respond. On the subway, he read from Baldwin, and one section appeared to speak directly to him in a manner that sent a cool shudder through his bloodstream. In this section the author spoke of how white society had pretty much expected nothing more than mediocrity from Black folks, and the idea of that affected him, troubled him.

He closed the book, slammed it closed really. He wondered if that was just what he had been doing for so long—making peace with mediocrity? And if so, wasn't he just playing along by the game plan the Man had lain out before him, leading him to a trap the way one led a rat to his doom with pieces of cheese? If this was true, then Stacie had been exactly right. By choosing to mire in the status quo, he was complicit in his own worthlessness. Had Rachel not just coddled him? Told him it was okay to not want more from his life? Whereas Stacie had challenged him, demanded he want more for himself. He clasped the book in his hands and looked around him. There were people of all nationalities and ethnicities with him on the train, and they all had one thing in common: they were all trying to get somewhere. They were all trying to fill the void. He made a note to himself—*Find out exactly where you are going and what it will take to get there.*

Fifteen

He had visited two states in his life. New Jersey hardly counted, but it was where a significant portion of his family lived and where he had spent a few memorable summers as a child at sleepaway camp. The other was Maryland. He'd driven there with his uncle when he was young, and it was memorable for its own reasons. When Rachel offered to pay for his ticket to come see her in Boston, he was both flattered and intrigued. He had always disliked Boston for sports rivalries, but the opportunity to be in a foreign setting with Rachel was too strong a draw.

He read his new Toni Morrison novel the whole trip, and as the train pulled into North Station, he could see Rachel from his seat. She was waiting on the platform, hands in her pockets, staring down. He could tell something was on her mind. She was wearing a large raincoat and no makeup, her hair pulled back in a messy ponytail. Her face looked sullen, distant. He was reminded that happiness was a most fleeting thing.

When they embraced, he instantly smelled marijuana and bourbon.

"How are you?" he asked.

"I'm good. It's been a crazy forty-eight hours. I'll explain at my place."

Her apartment was beyond sparse. There was a tiny kitchen area with a small table and two chairs. Her living room had a couch, a small

TV/VCR player, and a bookshelf with about two dozen books and a bunch of CDs. The door to her small balcony was open, airing out her minuscule bedroom. Unopened boxes marked *GLASSWARE* and *KIDS SCHOOLWORK* sat strewn across the floor. She made tea and they drank it at the table.

"I've been feuding with my therapist."

"What did the two of you feud about?"

"I have made the conscious choice to stop going to AA. I don't really have a lot in common with the people there. It's mostly whiny, screwed-up losers. I don't get a lot out of it."

"Well, if you don't get a lot out of it, then you should stop, right?"

"Makes sense, no? But no, Lydia thinks it is all part of a self-destructive pattern I've set myself on. She thinks that judging others helps me not look at myself."

"You're an adult, Rachel. You can make this decision on your own, right?"

"Yes, yes I can. Thank you. Can I tell you what else she thinks?" He followed her out to the balcony, where she lit a cigarette for the both of them. He waved her off; he was trying to quit again. "Aren't you Mr. Discipline? So, she also thinks that you are a part of my self-destructive pattern."

"Me?"

"Yes. She thinks I'm using you as part of some midlife crisis. To avoid responsibility."

"I'm sorry to hear that."

"Don't be. Do you know what I think? I think she is just jealous. She is jealous because I have found something that replenishes me. I have passion. I have fire. I am choosing, making a conscious choice to not allow darkness to quench my flame. And she is old and dry."

As she spoke, he watched her. He watched the way her hands darted around, the way her eyes, subtle purplish bags underlining them, resembled a frozen puddle. It occurred to him that he was quite possibly seeing a warped version of her, what remained of a flower that had sat in the overpowering sun for too long. The Rachel that he had come to adore wasn't fully there at this moment, and there was a part of him that mourned for her. But none of it mattered when she mashed out her cigarette and took his hand, leading him to her small twin bed. It was early afternoon, and they didn't leave her room until it was dark out.

They went to a Japanese restaurant in an old-fashioned neighborhood, Beacon Hill. Over sushi and Tokyo ramen, he did most of the listening, as usual. Michael was not making their separation easy, insisting that they give counseling another shot. Sebastian had been acting up in school lately, initiating fights with other kids and refusing to focus on assignments in class. It was possible the boy had attention deficit disorder. Hilary, the older one, seemed to be withdrawing from others. Maybe she was an introvert. Maybe she was emotionally damaged. Maybe she was just fiercely independent. It was hard to say. Both of her children's issues struck him as simply things that kids go through. He didn't see why either kid needed to see a mental-health professional. But he kept those thoughts to himself and chalked it up to "how white people deal with things."

She had a job interview with the University of Colorado in two weeks for a position in their music department, and then another later in the month with a university in Montreal. She was helping an old colleague work on a personal project, a chamber opera.

"What would you do if you got one of those jobs? How would that work with the kids and all?"

"It's a good question. They would move with me of course, and we'd have to work out some type of visitation arrangement."

"Do you think Michael would go for that?"

"He wouldn't have a choice. They're my children. I gave birth to them both."

"I know that, but I'm just saying, he has some rights, I imagine."

"He relinquished a lot of those rights when he slept with his first college student. I'm prepared to use whatever weapons I need to, Rashid. He knows I have his balls in a vise."

He couldn't keep up with her drinking. She was always two glasses ahead of him. In the taxi back to her place, she fell asleep on his shoulder. The taxi driver, a man close to his age, looked at him in the rearview mirror.

"That woman, she is your wife?" He had an accent from some part of Africa.

"My wife? No, she is my girlfriend."

"Your girlfriend? She is a bit older than you, yes?"

"Is that a problem?"

"No, no problem, brother. In America anything can happen."

The next day she took him to brunch at a trendy spot in the North End, and then they spent a couple of hours at the Museum of Fine Arts. At around three, they were drinking coffee in a café when she received a phone call. She stepped away from him to take it. He watched her talking on the phone in a familiar and overly expressive manner, swinging her arms and, from time to time, stomping her foot. He knew it could only be the husband. When she returned to him some fifteen minutes later, her face was crimson and sweat streaked across her forehead.

"I need to take care of something," she spit out. "Do you want to come with me or do you want to wait here?"

"I'll go with."

They drove to the YMCA. On the way, she explained that her son had been playing in his youth basketball league and had gotten into a fight with a referee. He'd been expelled from the game. The coach was insisting that one of the parents come pick him up, and Michael was claiming he had a migraine. When they reached the YMCA, the boy, still in uniform, was waiting outside with an assistant coach. His first impression of the kid was that he had the hostile and broken look of a person who will eventually grow up to be a bully, maybe even a serial killer. The boy climbed into the back seat, ignoring him, and though his mother tried to talk to him, he barely said three sentences all the way home.

He knew that Rachel came from money, but he was surprised at just how lavish and affluent the neighborhood that her family lived in was. As they drove down gorgeously tended streets, he craned his neck to take it all in. All around him were two- and three-story mini-mansions with huge well-manicured gardens and three-car garages. When they stopped at her former home, he stared in wonder at the extreme privilege. The boy got out without saying a word and ran inside. She told Rashid she would only be a few minutes and she ran in after him. As he sat there alone in the car, staring at the houses all around, a thought hit him: if aliens landed in that spot tomorrow and took over the earth, they would surmise that the majority of Black and brown people lived like ants, piled on top of one another in tall brick monstrosities in towns that smelled like trash and burnt-out death, while the majority of white people lived far away from all that in well-spaced houses with gardens, garages, and swimming pools. The idea of it caused his teeth to grind.

When Rachel finally emerged from the house, she had the exhausted look of a fighter who had gone a few rounds on an empty stomach. Without a word she started the car up and took off, nearly clipping a cat. Going through a new section of extravagant houses brought up Rashid's familiar feeling of resentment, but there was something else, something more that perturbed him about this experience with the son, and he couldn't hold it in any longer.

"So, what, I don't even merit an introduction?"

"Excuse me?" she replied, twirling her hair around her finger nervously.

"Your son. What am I, a Black ghost? It's like you don't even think I'm important enough for a basic 'Hey, this is your mom's friend Rashid?'"

"Unbelievable. Un-be-fucking-lievable! Do you have any idea how hard this is? Do you? Balancing a needy husband, a needy lover, two needy kids."

"Needy lover?"

"Sometimes it's hard to breathe, Rashid!" She slammed on the brakes right before going through a red light in a busy four-way intersection. "And what about you, huh? I don't see you rushing to invite me over for dinner with Mama James, now do I? You ever gonna get around to that?"

He laughed just a little. "You couldn't handle my neighborhood, Rachel. Trust me, it ain't nothing like this shit. I'm pretty sure you have no idea what the inside of any projects looks like, much less the projects in my hood."

"Nobody says we have to go to your neighborhood, Shid. I'd be happy to take your mom somewhere nice—Le Bernardin, Elaine's. Hell, I'd take her to KFC if that's what she wanted. But you don't really want that, do you? No, that might not mesh with your reputation. I'm not exactly the woman your mom dreamed you'd bring home, am I?"

He stared out at the traffic, suddenly impatient for her to move. His face was flush with heat. There was something about her KFC reference that didn't sit right with him.

"Yeah, see, you wanna have your cake and eat it too. I swear, you men are all the same. It's all about you."

"KFC, that was a nice touch there."

The rest of the ride back to her place was in silence. It was clear to him she had been drained by whatever took place back at the house. When they reached her apartment, she went straight out to the balcony and smoked a joint. There had been talk of them going to a Red Sox game at Fenway Park later on, but now she asked him to please be flexible with her and order food and watch the game from home. They ate Italian food from a local joint, drank wine by candlelight, and watched the game on her couch. In the middle of the sixth inning, the phone rang, and she answered it. He watched a repeat performance of the afternoon's phone call with her raging at the husband from the balcony for ten minutes. When the call was over, she threw her phone and stormed out of the room.

The hurled phone had knocked over a candle, and he watched in a detached manner for a few minutes as the flame from the candle caused a pile of magazines to go from a soft murmur to a full blaze. He knew he needed to act, but for whatever reason, he just sat there watching the orange glare. Years later he would look back at this incident and be amazed at how unaware he was of just what was taking place. His sheer ignorance would gnaw at him like a recurring migraine. Why did he not see it then? The unraveling—like so many strands of a finely threaded sateen blanket—was taking place right then and there every day. A thing he'd once thought was so beautiful was actually more of a mirage.

When she returned a few moments later, there was a strained vulnerability about her that seemed to come from a different place. She had been in the bathroom brushing her teeth, and several clumps of toothpaste spotted her blouse. Her eye makeup pooled down her cheeks, giving her face the look of a child's watercolor portrait. He had just placed the magazines in the kitchen sink and was running water over them when she walked up to him, clutching her left arm.

"Hey, I've got to go back to the house. Michael says he needs a time-out from Sebastian. I guess things got physical with them. I'm gonna have to bring him back here for the night."

"Okay. Do you want me to go to a hotel or something?"

"No, I don't want you to go to a hotel. I just wanted you to know. I'm really sorry about this."

"You don't have to apologize about your kids, Rachel. I get it. It isn't easy. I get it."

He went to her and the two held each other close. There was something foreign about her in the moment, which confounded him. It was like trying to embrace the rain.

"Do you wanna come with me to get him or just wait here?"

"I'll go with you. Sounds like you might need protection."

When they pulled up to the house, Rachel leaned over and stroked his face.

"This could take a little time. He might be resistant. If it's okay with you, I'd rather you wait here."

"Of course. I am gonna start smoking again, though. You got a cigarette?"

She smiled, handed him her pack, and they kissed briefly.

"You really are a good guy, you know that?"

He watched as she got out of the car and walked to the house, disappearing into the darkness of the rear garden. He got out, the night air inviting. He leaned against the car and watched all the houses around him for the second time in as many hours. At night the energy was a little different, but there was still a sense of great ease and tranquility there; he had the feeling that nothing bad could ever happen in a place like this. There was definitely not going to be a mugging or a drive-by shooting anytime soon. Probably never. He lit a cigarette and wondered what was going on inside the house.

The husband had walked out of the house at one point, and Rachel was right behind him. He had pointed at the car, at Rashid, and then went quickly back inside with her. He had appeared angry but feeble. His robe was undone and his hair disheveled. He had a small potbelly that protruded out of his T-shirt and hung out over his boxers like a half-filled water balloon. He had looked in Rashid's direction, but only briefly, as if he didn't want to give full existence to he who had become the new man in his wife's life. He thought about that phrase: *the new man*. Was that who he really was? Or was he in actuality the new *boy*? That was probably how the husband saw him. He dragged on the cigarette and waited, taking in the sounds of the evening.

He had a strong desire to approach the home, perhaps get up close to the door and listen in. Maybe he could gather some sense of what they were discussing. He had no doubt they were talking about him. Close to ten minutes had passed at this point. What could they possibly be discussing? He really wanted to know what was going on.

He lit a new cigarette and moved away from the car, closer to the house. He walked on the fresh, recently mown grass. Took it in, smelled it. He hadn't smelled anything like it since he was a child and he and Marlon had gone to that summer camp in New Jersey. Fresh-cut grass, with no glass, no dog shit, and no crack vials or hypodermic needles. What a luxury. He walked past a couple of white lawn chairs and what appeared to be a few cement balls and a mallet. He had heard of this game before, it was a French word. Parquet?

He moved across the grass to the lowest window he could find. He put his ear close, but heard nothing. He looked up and saw shadows moving in the upstairs window covered by a shade; an adult shadow and a smaller shadow appeared. He imagined one of them was talking to the son, Sebastian. *Who names kids Sebastian anymore?* He recalled the kid's face from the earlier car ride. The kid had looked at him only once, just like the father. It was like the both of them would prefer he never existed. In their world he didn't matter. In fact, in their world he was repulsive. He was the cockroach in the glass of milk.

He wished there were some way he could get upstairs, maybe there was a ladder? After scanning the area, he realized just how stupid that idea was and he walked back to the car. It had been close to fifteen minutes since Rachel had gone in the house, and he was starting to feel frustrated that she hadn't at least had the decency to come out and check on him. He wondered what Stacie would have thought of the whole situation. She would have been ashamed of him, called him a fool. He made a mental note to give Rachel shit about this type of behavior. He deserved better.

He was fishing his third cigarette from his pocket when the car slowly approached him. It was black and white, pristine, like a sleek polar bear. The candy-colored blue and red lights atop it were not flashing, but the vehicle still wielded a distinct sense of menace and authority. It was an image that was recognizable in any town and any city in any state. His first thought was that perhaps Rachel had called the police on her husband; perhaps things had gotten ugly. But the flashlight from the passenger side was shining directly on him, and that was when it hit—someone had called the cops on *him*.

The officer with the flashlight got out first. He had a youthful face, boyish even. Rashid gathered the guy was probably a rookie. He was white and clear skinned, like the member of a popular boy band. He felt safe with this kid approaching his left side. It was his partner Rashid kept his eye on, the chiseled veteran, no doubt, who emerged from the driver's side and walked slowly towards him with the casual grace of a lazy wrestler. The older man had a ridiculously full mustache and large brown eyes that reminded him of a psychopath he had once seen on an old television movie—the one who led that cult that killed all of them rich white folks in California in 1969. Manson, that was it. This cop coming up on his right resembled Charles Manson with a crew cut. Manson did all the talking.

"How's it going?"

"It's going alright. You?"

"It's going good. Got a report that we gotta check out, ya know? You mind telling us what you're up to wandering around this area this time of night?"

He looked below the man's badge where the word "Payton" rested.

"I wasn't wandering around, officer. I'm waiting for a friend."

"A friend, huh? Where might this friend be?"

"She lives in this house."

"This house, huh? Hey, buddy, you got some ID on you?"

"Have I committed a crime, officer?"

"Now, let's not jump to any conclusions. Nobody is saying you committed any crime. We just have a job to do, and I hope that you'll respect that job."

Rashid looked at the rookie, who had sympathetic eyes and gave the impression that he was ashamed to be there at the moment. Below his badge, it read, "Bertrand."

"I'm sorry, but I don't have any ID on me, it's back at my friend's place."

"Friend's place, huh? I thought this was your friend's place."

Rashid's mouth started going a little dry. His tongue felt heavier than it normally did.

"My friend has two places . . . Listen, I haven't done anything wrong."

"Oh, your friend has two places, huh? Why don't you come with us for a moment?"

"I haven't committed any crime. I know my rights."

"He knows his rights, Jason. Oooh! What, we got a Harvard Law student, here? We got Johnnie Cochran Jr. over here? Why don't you tell us what your friend's name is, buddy? The one who lives here."

Manson took out his notepad while the rookie answered the radio attached to his vest. Rashid heard him say, "We have confronted the suspect. We're currently in discussion."

He reached for a cigarette.

"Whoa, whoa, easy there, buddy." Manson had his hand on Rashid's hand now.

"I'm getting a cigarette."

"Okay, let's communicate that, alright? Let's be careful about all of this. I'm telling you right now, it would behoove you to not make any unnecessary sudden movements."

"I was getting a cigarette."

"So, clearly I'm not getting through to you."

Just then the door to the house opened, and Rachel, son behind her carrying a knapsack, walked across the lawn towards them. At first she looked at them all bewildered, a moment that transformed quickly into anger. She approached Manson.

"What is going on here?"

"Ma'am, I take it you reside here?"

"Yes, I *reside* here. I have for fourteen years now. What is this about?"

"Ma'am, we had a report of a suspicious party lurking in the area. I take it you know this individual?"

He noted how Manson's tone had taken on a new quality. He was no longer the intimidator, the authoritarian.

She looked at Rashid, and in a move that utterly surprised him, she took his hand in hers.

"This *individual* is my boyfriend, thank you, officer. I had no idea it was a crime to have your boyfriend wait outside while you gathered your things."

He noted the use of "boyfriend." He had never heard her use it with him before, and he felt a mixture of confusion and pride surge within. He looked to the son, who met his gaze with equal bafflement.

"Your boyfriend, really? Looks like you did alright for yourself, Johnnie Cochran."

"What does that—what are you saying to him?"

"Nothing, ma'am, nothing. Can I just get your name for my report?"

"No, you can't get my name for your report. There is nothing here for you to report."

"Well, it looks like our work is done here. Nothing for us to be concerned about." Manson tipped his hat to them, and both of the officers headed back to the vehicle. Rashid could tell she wasn't quite ready to be done with it all. He watched as she left his side and walked to the car.

"You know, you can't just show up and intimidate someone with your badge because you think they look like they don't belong somewhere."

"Ma'am, we were just doing our job. We had a report of a possible disturbance, and it's our job to investigate these matters. This was clearly a false report, and we will now be on our way. You have yourself a good evening."

Manson nodded in Rashid's direction, giving him a subtle wink that seemed to say, "Until we meet again."

They all watched as the car took off into the brightly moonlit night, slinking away like a boa constrictor, post devouring.

"My fucking tax dollars at work," she said to no one in particular.

That night, the son slept on the couch, and he and Rachel slept in the bedroom with the door partially open. The next morning, he watched her get up much earlier than she normally did, and he listened to her and the son talking over making pancakes. To his surprise, the son turned out to be pretty nice, calm. When Rashid appeared from the bedroom wearing his sweatpants and a Knicks jersey, the son rolled his eyes and made fun of the Knicks. It set off an amusing back-and-forth between them over sports rivalries, favorite sports heroes, and eventually music tastes. The son leaned towards heavy metal and classic rock, but also had an appreciation for hip hop. Rashid watched Rachel beam with what he assumed was a mixture of happiness and relief as she handed him his second mug of coffee and kissed his forehead.

They took Sebastian out to Fenway Park for an afternoon game and then to an early dinner at a hamburger chain afterward. "Hey, I'm sorry for yesterday," the kid said, sipping hard on his soda.

"What are you sorry about?"

"I don't know. I think I was rude to you."

"No problem, kid. You had a lot going on, I imagine."

"My school counselor says I have anger issues. You ever have anger issues?"

The sincere honesty of the question coming from the kid struck him, and he paused before responding. An image of him and Darnell as kids was slowly coming back to him. In his recollection Darnell had refused to give him back the joystick during a computer game they had been playing. Darnell was lying back on the floor, holding it at arm's length, taunting him. He did the only thing he could think to do—he rose and smashed his foot down on Darnell's arm. His brother screamed.

"I have had anger issues, yes. I don't know anyone who is human who hasn't."

"Well, I'm sorry. I didn't mean to take it out on you."

He watched the boy shove fries into his mouth, and the care that he felt for the boy stunned him.

They took Sebastian back to the house after dinner, and the two of them slapped hands and fist-bumped goodbye. As he watched Rachel walk arm and arm with him back into the house, he leaned back in his seat and went into her purse for a pack of cigarettes. He thought to step outside to have a smoke, but last night's experience with the cops stayed close to him and he smoked from inside. A few minutes later Rachel came back out and got in the car.

"Well, well, didn't you just charm the pants off my boy?"

"What can I tell you? I have skills."

"He really liked you, ya know?" She grabbed the cigarette from his mouth and took a drag.

"Maybe we should do the daughter tomorrow."

"Whoa, whoa, easy there. If you thought he was a tough nut to crack . . . I bet you were an easygoing child, weren't you?"

"Oh, I don't know about that. My mom might have a different opinion on that topic."

"Come on, we both deserve a few drinks after this day."

They went to a local pub two blocks from her apartment. As was usual, he could not keep up with her. After her fourth shot of whisky, "Sexual Healing" started up on the jukebox, and she invited him to dance, claiming, "Hey, this is our jam!" They joined a few other couples on the floor, all white, and he could feel himself struggling to hold her up, she was so inebriated. Still, he was happy to be there with her, happy to be alone with her.

"You know, your son made me think of something today."

"Oh yeah, what's that? That you never wanna have kids?"

"No, no, not that at all. He was talking to me about his anger issues. He asked me if I have anger issues."

"Do you? I don't think you do."

"I don't think I do either. But he got me thinking, I am very angry at my brother."

"Oh yeah? Why, he try to fuck your girlfriend?"

The brusqueness of her tone took him aback, and although she tried to laugh it off, he found himself disappointed. The couple next to them had overheard her, and they were giving him a strange look. He turned back to her.

"What the—"

"I'm sorry, bad joke. Bad joke, baby."

"Why would you say that?"

"It's a thing, you know. Some brothers try to fuck each other's girlfriends. It happens."

"You're drunk, Rachel. You're drunk again."

"Hey, hey, don't be that way. I'm not drunk. I'm just enjoying myself after a somewhat challenging day. Don't call me drunk."

"Rachel."

"Shhhh." She kissed him. "Don't talk. You're much more fun when you dance."

A sadness took ahold of him as he looked around her bedroom the next morning. They had woken each other up to make love, and she was in bed playing the flute. The shades were drawn so that only a tiny blade of sunlight came into the room. The walls were bare and gray, like the inside of a coffin.

"Why don't you put anything up on your walls?"

"I was gonna get around to it. I think I'll put my Monet over on that wall."

"Serious. I think it would brighten the mood in this place."

"I grew up in a house with an artist. We had fine art everywhere. It didn't make us any happier."

"Are you going to be cynical forever?"

"Am I going to be cynical forever? I don't know that I can answer that question just now. Hey, do you recognize this?"

He sat back and listened as she played a few bars of a song that was familiar, but he couldn't quite place it. He watched her features. There was something lovely and placid about her when she played the flute. Her eyes remained closed most of the time, but every now and then, he caught her looking up to him, as if she wanted his approval. He understood all over again just how he had come to fall in love with her. Sure, she had demons. She had weaknesses. Her art was a way to bury all of it, if only for a brief while. He envied her like he envied Muriel with her talent. Perhaps he could find an art form that could console him. What was his talent, he wondered?

"I do kinda. What is it?"

"Silly. It's the Jackson Five, 'I'll Be There.' Jesus, how young are you again?"

"Young enough for my Black ass to know better."

"Why don't you take that young Black ass over to the kitchen and make me some coffee?"

"Yes, Miss Daisy," he replied in an exaggerated Southern drawl. "Will missus like one lump or two?"

They spent the afternoon unpacking some of her boxes while listening to a compilation of classical music. At one point he stumbled upon an old mustard-colored photo album. On the cover, written in clumsy script, were the words *July Wedding, 1982*. He looked around and saw that she was stacking books on a bookshelf in the bedroom. He flipped through the first pages of the album. A much younger Rachel in tight blue jeans and a pink tank top poses in front of a fountain, blowing a kiss at the camera. Younger Rachel, her parents, and the husband dine in a classy restaurant, all dressed up. At different moments various people are toasting the young couple. He realized this must be shortly before the wedding. The next several pages were all wedding photos. The happy couple, white gown and black tuxedo, stand before a crowd at an outdoor ceremony, a female officiant between them. The couple cutting the cake later that night. In another she is smearing his face with wedding cake, and everyone around them laughs in that phony way people always seem to laugh at this moment. The couple boarding a horse-drawn carriage and taking off from the scene. The next several pages were all pictures from an exotic-looking tropical island. She wears a striped bikini. He looks skinny and pale in boxers. A waiter serving them drinks by the pool looks Latino.

He couldn't figure out why in the moment, but something about seeing how happy Rachel once was dug at his chest, a slow gnawing. He wondered how something that looked and seemed so right could ever go so wrong. *Where did this effortlessly smiling Rachel go?* Did he make her this happy? Could he ever? He closed the album when he heard her calling him into the bedroom. She wanted his help adding another level to the bookshelf. As she held the plank in place, he screwed in each end.

"Can I ask you a question?" he said.

"Why do you always do that?"

"Do what?"

"Ask me if you can ask me a question? Just ask the question!"

"Fine. What made you fall in love with Michael?"

"Whoa. Where did that come from?"

"I unpacked one of your photo albums. Your wedding one."

"Ah, I see. How about that hair of mine back then, huh?"

"It was something."

"Hey, it was all the rage. You don't know who Farrah Fawcett was, do you?"

"A model?"

"Something like that."

"You gonna answer my question?"

"I am. Why did I fall in love with Michael? Well, like you, he had a certain charm about him, a grace and an elegance in how he handled himself. How he moved through the world. I've always been drawn to men who have a quietness about them that holds a strength within it. And he was a very talented musician. I'm a fan of Emily Dickinson, and after our second date, he took one of her poems and put it to music for me. It was unique and it was special. I found out years later of course that it was a thing he did with several of his girlfriends—compose cheap little pieces for them, intended to melt their hearts and their panties all the same. It's amazing how unique and special can quickly transform into tawdry and disingenuous."

"You looked pretty happy in those wedding photos."

"I was happy. Nineteen eighty-two was quite the year, not as eventful as 1981. In '81, I had been watching Princess Diana and Prince Charles's wedding on TV at home, and we were all just lounging around eating cucumber sandwiches and drinking Earl Grey tea in celebration. My father got up to make himself a brandy, when all of a sudden he fell hard down on his knees, clutching his chest. He was having a heart attack, his first, and we had to rush him to the hospital. We took a taxi, we were so afraid an ambulance wouldn't arrive in time. He was in intensive care for about a week, and Michael was there every day to hold my hand and help me through it. I was so afraid I was gonna lose my dad. I was so afraid. Michael earned my trust during that dark time, and though he eroded it years later, I will never forget how safe I felt with him back then."

"I would like to keep you safe someday."

"You do, babe. Trust me, you do. It's part of why I love you now. I want to keep you safe too. I fear I'm not doing a very good job of that."

He felt the warmth of her palm on his cheek. He placed his hand atop hers.

"He's given you things that I could never give you."

"And you've given me things he could never give me."

"Yeah? Like what?"

"Like what? A twenty-five-year-old lay for one."

He huffed so hard that both of them erupted in belly-shaking laughter, which then led to hugging, embracing, stroking, and an eventual return to the bed that had been covered with old albums.

That night they went to a wineshop in her neighborhood. Every Sunday was movie night there, and on this night they showed *The King and I*. He had never seen it before. They watched in a crowd of about twenty others, all of them white. It made him feel good to have her reach out to hold his hand during the opening credits. By the time the lights came up for the closing credits, Rachel had fallen asleep. He noticed she had easily drunk about five glasses of wine during the course of the film.

When he approached the cashier to pay, Rachel stopped him and pulled out her credit card.

"Uh-uh. You provide the sex, I pay," she told him.

He and the cashier shared an awkward smile. On the walk home she asked him what he thought of the film. When he told her that he liked it alright but wished it had a happier ending, she scoffed.

"Happy endings are for saps."

"Consider me a sap then."

"I'm sorry, but we don't all get to wake up from the nightmare back in our warm bed in Kansas."

"I guess not."

"Do you think we'll have a happy ending?"

"I certainly hope so. Don't you?"

"If life has anything to say about it, I highly doubt it."

Before he knew what was happening, she had grabbed his hands and started a poorly executed waltzing movement around the sidewalk, all the while humming the chorus to one of the popular songs in the movie. He recognized it as the one in which the regal, bald-headed king grabs his lovely leading lady and starts swooshing around the floor with her. He played along, realizing what she was doing and actually enjoying the moment until she danced herself into a garbage can, knocking it over and falling to the ground in the process. He watched her as she lay there on the ground, as if she were pondering the situation. As he looked around them, he saw that some of the people nearby were looking at him with concern, as if he had in some way done something to harm her.

"Rachel, get up."

"I kinda like it down here."

He said it more forcefully. "Rachel, get up!" He reached down and attempted to pull her up, but she resisted, slapping his hands away.

"Fuck off! I get up when I say I get up. Keep your paws off me."

"Jesus Christ, Rachel. You're such a drunk."

"Watch it, okay? Just watch it. I won't be insulted by some waiter from Brooklyn."

A young couple who were passing by with their grocery bags looked over at him suspiciously, then went to her.

"Miss, can we help you in some way?" the man asked.

"Fuck off, yuppie scum. I'm waiting for my boyfriend over there to ask me to get up nicely."

They looked at him again. He walked away.

In the morning, they were quiet over breakfast for a good ten minutes. As she poured him a second cup of coffee, she leaned over and kissed him.

"Listen," she said. "I'm . . . I'm gonna go back to AA. I promise." She kissed his hand. He kissed her hand and her cheek as she sat in his lap. "I sort of don't know what's happening with me, Shid."

She drove him to the train station. He had been going over something in his mind the entire trip, and he was determined to bring it up to her. As the train conductor announced the final boarding, he kissed her. She zipped his jacket.

"I'll be back in the city in about a month, maybe sooner."

"Hey, I have an idea: Why don't you just move to the city? Get a teaching job there. We can get a place together."

Her response was much less enthusiastic than he had expected.

"Get a place together?"

"Yeah, I'm looking to get out of my mom's place. Two salaries are better than one."

"Do you have any idea how that would look? Should I just forget I have two kids here?"

"You said if you got a job in another state, you would have to make arrangements. Is that not still the case?"

"Hey, listen. Let's take this one day at a time, okay?"

"Forget I ever brought it up."

"Think, Rashid, think about what you're proposing here. Think about how that would look to people in your life."

He boarded the train and sat by the window. He was troubled by that statement. Did she mean to say, "Think about how that would look to people in your life," or did she mean to say, "Think about how that would look to people in *my* life"?

She was standing there outside his train window, arms crossed. He saw her face, the look of someone who had just been broadsided by a gust of wind. He had thought—hoped—she would have been moved and flattered by his offer. It bothered him that he could be so wrong about so many things. He waved goodbye to her as the train took off, unclear just when he would ever see her again.

Sixteen

Rashid decided to focus on cooking. He had been watching the kitchen staff for months now, and he often found himself intrigued by the sweaty men with aprons, hats, and five-o'clock shadows, who labored over boiling pots, greasy pans, and sizzling grills all day long. There was one woman on the crew, Natalie, but she only came in on weekends. He put all his energy into closely monitoring the one crew member he knew best: head chef Mario Debanadetti. Mario was a confident man who gave as good as he got. He was forty-four years old, and he had a Black boyfriend named Leonard who was a nurse at NYU Medical Center.

After some light nudging, Lucia had agreed to let him work in the kitchen one night a week. Any additional time he desired was his to take, but it would have to be unpaid, which was fine for him. He appreciated the lessons and Mario's willingness to take him under his wing. He worked in the kitchen during his Monday shift, and came in on Saturdays to observe.

Mario proved to be a good teacher and Rashid proved to be a quick study. He grew to love many of the tasks and details associated with meal preparation. Deboning chicken; seasoning beef and veal; chopping garlic and onions, parsley and basil; sautéing bell peppers; making homemade pasta—the flour, the eggs, the kneading of the dough. He learned that when cooking meatballs, moisture was everything; that the meat should be moist, not soggy; and that eggs could help bind the meatballs together. It was much harder work than he had imagined; it took strong hands. He developed an appreciation for eggplant he had never had before. Antony gifted him a cast-iron skillet, and he practiced at home on his grateful mother. Mario was so full of knowledge that Rashid was amazed the man wasn't the host of his own cooking show.

"You want the eggplant to be like a succulent woman," Mario told him. "Not too thin, not too thick slices."

"As if you know," a cook sniped.

"Ignore that idiot," Mario went on. "Deep-fry it on a high heat. Don't smother it. Give it space."

"Also like a woman," Rashid replied, wiping sweat from his brow.

All his life he had used butter in the very few dishes he knew how to make. With Mario he learned that olive oil was one of the greatest ingredients ever gifted by God.

"A chef without olive oil," Mario told him, "is like a painter without a brush."

It took him about a month and a half to feel comfortable making a meal on his own. Rashid very much enjoyed cooking for his mother. He even went over to Marlon's apartment and cooked for him and his girlfriend, who was pregnant with their second child, but he was most anxious to impress Rachel. He got his first opportunity when she came for a visit while her brother was out of town. In the brother's kitchen, Rashid made chicken with white beans and tomato sauce, while Rachel looked on from the table, pouring them regular glasses of wine and occasionally kissing him from behind on the neck as he labored over the stove.

A compilation CD played in the background, and when "Once in a Blue Moon" came on, he stopped everything to dance with her. Cooking for her made him feel masculine, and the aroma of oregano, garlic, and roasted chicken was intoxicating. Later that night, they broke a leg of the brother's couch with their ferocious lovemaking.

He hoped this passion was the sign of a glorious weekend to come for them, but the next morning came with clouds. Her job interviews had not panned out as she had hoped, and she was convinced there was an ugly force working against her. Over hard-boiled eggs and gourmet coffee, she shared her thoughts about how she believed certain former composers she had worked with had made up stories about her and were giving her poor recommendations because she was perceived as difficult in some circles.

She knew one of the people who had been hired for a teaching position she sought in Cincinnati, and it angered her. She was certain the woman had been hired because she was Hispanic. She claimed she was the victim of reverse discrimination. Rashid couldn't believe his ears, and he bit his tongue at first. He knew better than to disagree with her when she was this heated. Then at one point, when she kept going on about it, he couldn't help himself.

"I mean, I'm telling you, in today's climate, in some occupations, you are better off with the name Hernandez than Hirschenfeld, you know?"

"Give me a break, Rachel. Is it at all possible that she was just better suited for the job?"

The velocity with which she rose from the table caused his mug to tip over and spill.

"I guess I should have expected that."

"It's just, you know, I have a hard time listening to that nonsense. People like you and your husband, your brother, you have all been the beneficiaries of discrimination for generations. It's not gonna crush my soul because once in a blue moon a brown person gets something one of you guys wanted."

"No, no, of course not. And why should you care? You're right. You have every reason to receive everything. People who looked like my great-great-grandfather brought your great-great-grandmother over here on a ship. All that horrible shit. It's only fair that I suffer for it some three hundred years later."

One afternoon Rachel went to spend time with her mother while Rashid went to work. They planned to meet up later in the evening at the brother's house, and for the sake of convenience, she had given him his own key to the place. He got to the apartment early and excitedly started his preparations to make veal marsala. In the bathroom, he was sitting on the toilet, and he looked down in the wastebasket at something off that had caught his eye. He reached down and picked up a used syringe, the blood on the tip of the needle still fresh crimson. He put his nose to it, and it reeked of vinegar and salt. He dug deeper in the basket and saw that there were three other needles in there as well as a few rubber tourniquets. His breath shortened and anxiety filled his lungs. He wondered how it could be he had never noticed anything before. He'd just thought she was drinking too much, stressed with family and work, maybe a little stoned now and then.

When she arrived at the apartment an hour later, she looked haggard. It was at that moment he realized what a fool he'd been.

"It smells great in here," she said. He pulled back as she went to kiss him. "Hey, what's up?"

"You tell me. How was your day?"

"Oh, you know. Full day with the Great Whiner. Bound to tire anyone out. How are you? You seem tense."

"I found something. Something I think you left behind."

He produced the syringe from a drawer, and then watched her face. He could see the wheels spinning.

"Where did you get that?"

"It was in the bathroom in the garbage. There were a few of them."

"Huh. Must be my brother's."

"Your brother hasn't been here in weeks, Rachel. This was clearly used recently. Like hours ago."

He watched her face transform as if she were looking into a fun-house mirror.

"Maybe his cleaning lady, then. You don't think that's me, do you?"

"Can I see your purse?"

"My purse, why?"

"Can I see it, please?" He held out his hand. She pulled her purse closer to her chest, looking terrified and protective.

"No. I'm not gonna be interrogated."

She went to move away, but he grabbed her by the wrist. Their eyes locked, and he felt his patience oozing from his pores as she struggled to hold on to what were clearly the last threads of her fabrication.

"You don't understand, Rashid."

"What don't I understand?"

"Everything that made me feel important, gave me meaning, I have lost. Everything."

She threw the purse at him. When he went to pick it up, she hurled herself at him and into his arms.

"I'm losing everything!" she cried.

"You're not losing everything," he said as gravity pulled them to the floor. "I'm here, Rachel."

"You won't be forever. I know you won't."

"What are you talking about?"

"Don't you think I know that I'm on the clock here?"

The night was hard. After much prolonged silence spent sitting on the couch, she fell asleep. He watched her, stroked her hair, put on music. He was restless. He went out to take a walk, and when he returned, she was asleep in bed, still fully dressed. He watched television on the couch and fell asleep there. In the morning, he made them coffee. They talked briefly, awkwardly. She asked him to go get them bagels from a favorite place a few blocks away. When he returned with the bagels, she was gone. There was a note:

*I'm gonna head to my mother's, spend the afternoon with
her. Then gonna head home a couple of days early. I will
call you. I'm so sorry. I've fucked up in so many ways,
Rashid. Please be patient with me.*

He folded the note, showered, and went home. In his room he played
his flute. His mother popped her head in to check on him. He told her
he was fine, just overworked. She left him to his solitude. He was realizing things. His lover, who he thought he knew so well, was actively
shooting heroin into her veins. His lover was actively doing the thing
that had brutally killed his father. There was much more at play than
the drinking problem he had assumed was her main issue. And to add
to it, she had lied to his face in an effort to cover it up. And the speed
with which she'd lied to him. Then she had bawled like a six-year-old.
He recalled something he had seen on a documentary about drug addic-
tion once. The narrator had spoken about how the addict, at the height
of their disease, could be a great manipulator, would do or say just about
anything to maintain their habit. It was something anyone who'd grown
up in Bed Stuy knew from the neighborhood, but the truth of it hadn't
really hit him until that moment. A disturbing question kept reinserting
itself: *Who is Rachel, really?*

At Comforti's, a group of well-dressed Black women, all college
aged, entered and sat at his table. It was the birthday of the young
woman at the head of the table. She was very pretty, lean like a long-
distance track runner, eyes overexaggerated and deep brown like a doll's.
The group stayed about two hours, did not tip exceedingly well, and
left half-drunk. On the receipt, the birthday girl had written, *I like
your style. I'm a student at Fordham. If you ever want to get a drink, call.
Bernadette.* She had included a phone number. He had noticed a slight
flirtation on his visits to the table, but a lot of customers got that way
after a couple of drinks. He put the note in his locker.

Over the next couple of weeks, he went on with his normal life, but every day, he checked his phone, hoping he would hear from Rachel. In the middle of the third week, he broke down while walking past Padrinos and he called her. She picked up on the third ring. She sounded genuinely happy to hear from him, but exhausted.

"I just wanted to see how things were going for you. I miss you."

"Oh, Shid, I miss you too. Things are what they are. My car got towed, impounded. My license had been suspended after my DUI. I thought I could get away with a trip here and there. Not the case."

"That sounds awful. How are you getting around?"

"Hey, that's why God invented taxis, right?"

He heard in her the fatigued tone of forced laughter from a slowly fading heart.

"How's the job search?"

"Honestly? I've just about given up. The current reality is I can't move anywhere that's going to take me too far from the kids. I've applied for a few high school positions here in the area. One of those should pan out. How are you? How is your cooking?"

"It's good. I'm in the kitchen two nights a week now. You should taste my manicotti casserole. Say, are you up for a visit? I'd be happy to hop on the train."

"Shid . . ." There was a long silence, within which he sensed something dreadful approaching. It was similar to waiting for the imposing boom of thunder after a lightning flash. "I've made a difficult decision."

"What is it?"

"This is my last week in this apartment. I'm moving back home. The kids really need me."

"The kids. I see."

"Yeah, I think it would be healthy for them. I've been selfish, Shid. This has been harder on them than I ever imagined."

"I see. I understand. So it's just for the kids?"

"Yeah, pretty much."

"So you're not gonna share a bed with Michael again?"

"Oh god, Shid. You don't understand."

There was a long moment of silence as he watched his train go by across the street, the way passengers loaded and unloaded like the robots in a video game. It saddened him to think in a few minutes he would be one of them, moving passionless through the grid.

"I have no idea how long it will last."

"When were you planning on telling me this, Rachel? Like, if I hadn't just caved in and called you today, when would you have told me? When you were already back home? Why wouldn't you reach out to me about something like this?"

"I don't know. I think I was a little afraid. This is all so . . ."

He hung up.

That night, he had planned to cook for Marlon and his second girlfriend, Stefani, at her apartment two projects over from his. It was a funny arrangement, and he struggled mightily to figure out how Marlon made the threesome work, but each woman knew about the other and both seemed content with the arrangement for the time being. In fact, Stefani was trying to get pregnant too, and Marlon had hoped that this gesture of a romantic evening with a "hired chef" would do the trick and get them on the path to babyhood. To hear Marlon tell it, it was "all about negotiation, baby. When cooler heads can prevail and talk things out like reasonable adults, anything can happen. They need to send my Black ass over to the Gaza Strip."

He and Marlon roamed the aisles of the grocery store, picking up ingredients for the meal, a simple rigatoni with vodka sauce. Rashid couldn't hold in his anger and disappointment, and he shared his earlier conversation with Rachel.

"It sounds like she's in a dark place."

"Sigmund fucking Freud over here. No shit, man, but what about me? Like, don't my feelings have any say in this? Don't you think she owed me some type of explanation? Some type of communication?"

"No, you're right. That definitely would have been nice. But can I ask you a question?" They stopped to inspect a couple of broccoli heads. "Where did you see all of this going?"

"What do you mean? Like big picture?"

"Yeah, like big picture, nigga. Like, in the story of your mind, how did this movie end? The two of you walk off into the sunset riding on a horse with, like, Whitney Houston singing over the credits and shit? I mean, it seems to me like that wasn't anywhere near the reality of y'all's situation. From the very beginning you knew she had a husband and kids. Did you think those characters would just disappear? What, were you hoping the husband would get a composing job in Tokyo and take the kids and leave her behind so the two of you could just be on your own together?"

Rashid picked up a bottle of wine and looked at the label while Marlon's words danced around in his head. It felt a little like déjà vu; he'd had this conversation with Rachel already. Perhaps she had warned him all along and he had just been too dense to get it.

"I guess I just thought, hoped, that she would be up front with me."

"Yeah, well, sometimes that shit is easier said than done. Sometimes feeling things and saying things—they are like from two different planets. Sometimes shit can take months, years, to travel from your heart to your tongue. For some people it never happens. You think my arrangement with Zelda and Stefani came easy? Shit, this was months and months of me kinda flailing and trying to figure shit out. And during it all, I was one duplicitous motherfucker. I'm lucky this shit's actually worked out as well as it has, though I'm still not sure that one night one of these sisters ain't gonna straight up knife me in the back while I'm sleeping. This is the price we pay, the penance for daring to love outside the rules. We've always known this. If you don't like it, there's another way. You can always take a vow of chastity, become a priest. Which, of course has its own complications.

Stacie's musical was in its second week of rehearsals at a small theatre in Hoboken. Rashid had been on the list of a few select people she'd asked to come view the sessions and provide feedback. He took the afternoon ferry from a pier in downtown Manhattan. On the ferry he sat on a bench, just staring at the water. There was an undeniable beauty in viewing the city from the middle of the Hudson River on a summer day. A few feet away from him sat a little girl, no older than ten or eleven. The woman with her was white, and the girl, clearly the woman's daughter based on appearance, was an impeccable light brown with thick, neat dreadlocks. The father had to be Black. The girl was comfortably, intently engrossed in a book, while her mother read from a newspaper. At one point, the girl leaned over and asked her mother a question about the book. The mother responded to her briefly, and the two went back to their respective material. It occurred to him that if he and Rachel had a daughter, she would look very much like this girl. When the ferry docked, and the girl and her mother eventually walked away from him, he felt a sadness not unlike grief.

There were five actors working on Stacie's production, but in his opinion, only one was exceptional. The actress who played Nina Simone's daughter, Lisa, had not just an exquisite singing voice, but an impassioned and vulnerable portrayal. He knew that regardless of where this show went, the actress should have a successful, productive career. He expected to see her name somewhere down the line.

Kenya was there, and the two of them sat together in the small auditorium, writing notes on a document Stacie had drawn up herself. Kenya, too, had found the actress profoundly moving, and the two of them compared their notes in the lobby at the end of the show. Kenya looked healthy and happy.

"The dude playing the husband, Andy," she said. "He really can't sing. Also, he's got this really annoying tendency to mouth the words of the other actors onstage."

"I noticed that. What do you think of the actor who played her piano teacher?"

"Not a great actor, but effective. And beautiful to look at. Rumor has it, Stacie is fucking him."

"Get out of here. That dude?"

"It's what I heard. But you know, my source is pretty sketchy, so I wouldn't go putting that out there just yet."

At the bar later that night, Stacie vehemently denied the romance as Rashid sat with her on an outside balcony drinking scotch and beer.

"First of all, it would be terribly unprofessional. Now, if he looked like Wesley Snipes, then I might be willing to risk that. But I thought I made it clear to you—I don't do white boys."

"Oh, come on now. You're not being fair. What about that German dude you were with when you were at Penn State?"

"Oh my god, you gonna harp on the one white guy I ever experimented with. Okay, yes, I was with Justin Vogelsang for, like, a semester."

"Yeah, and was it really all that horrible?"

"No, no, it wasn't. He was actually really nice, and his family was nice too."

"Okay, so then what's the big deal?"

"The big deal is it was weird. It's hard to articulate, but I remember there was this time I went over to his house for a couple of days over Thanksgiving break, and his family was so sweet to me. And I recall thinking, *Wow, it is so great that these people accept me for who I am.* But in retrospect, what I was really saying was, *Wow, isn't it great that these people still like me even though I'm Black as night.* I was playing a fucked-up self-esteem game, and I think a lot of Black and brown people do this. And not just us. You know, I read somewhere that many Asian cultures are really fucked up too. For them, they grew up with white-American celebrity culture rammed down their throats by the media to the point where, for a lot of young women, their ideal male is not one of their own. Their ideal mate is a blond-haired, blue-eyed surfer dude. The ideal mate for a high school girl in Tokyo or South Korea is fucking Brad Pitt."

"Where do you come up with this shit?"

"I read. I manage a bookstore. What you think?"

"What's up with Kenya? She's looking kinda good."

"Of course she's looking good. Homegirl leads a healthy lifestyle. All vegan and shit."

"I was thinking about giving her a call later this week."

"I wouldn't if I were you."

"Why not?"

"Y'all are too much, man. What, you think she just sat around waiting for your Black ass to get your shit together? She been done moved on. She's fucking this yoga instructor from Washington Heights."

Seventeen

Rashid watched the heavy and violent downpour from the safety of the subway platform. As a child, he was always fascinated by thunderstorms; the sense that at any moment, you could be swept away by nature's wrath like in that section of the Bible that always seemed like a silly cartoon to him, the one that had the animals going two by two into the large boat. He had regarded that book as a fable even back then, but the hostility of storms and the potential of chaos always stayed with him. The idea of a fresh new start was not without its appeal. Every time the rain subsided, he felt the slightest disappointment that life as he knew it would continue.

It was late in the summer, that depressing time when it was starting to get darker earlier. When his phone rang, he was sure it would be his mother. He was running late for their dinner date. But the number was Rachel's. He hadn't seen it for months. He gathered his emotions, then answered it.

"Hello," he said, suppressing his anxiety.

"Hello," she responded. "I wasn't sure you would answer."

"Why wouldn't I?" He was like an actor. He could win an award for his poise alone. "What can I do for you, Rachel?"

"I sent you a letter about a week ago. It just came back to me. Did I get Comforti's address wrong?"

"I don't know. I'm not at Comforti's anymore." He was lying. He had received the envelope, smelled it, taken in her penmanship, and then written *RETURN TO SENDER* across the top. "I got a new job at a place in Queens managing a coffee shop." This was actually Marlon's life.

"Oh. Well, change is nice I suppose. Can I send it to your home?"

"I don't want it, Rachel. I really just want to move on. This part of my life . . ."

"I get it. I do. I told you that you would hate me one day."

"I don't hate you, Rachel. Trust me. It's just . . . it's easier to forget."

"Of course. I don't want to forget, though. You brought so much joy to my life, Shid. When things were good with us, there was no one who brought me more happiness. It just wasn't built to last. We both know there was a gulf between us—oceans really. It would always be there."

"Is that what your letter said?"

"It said a lot, Shid. It was, like, eight pages."

He looked down and heaved in the smell of fresh rain on the platform.

"What do you think that gulf was, Rachel?"

"You know what it was. It was always there. Always will be. It's written in blood on every Black face and white face in America. My ancestors did unspeakable things to your ancestors not so long ago. It left a wound that will infect us all forever. I tried to say so much in my letter. I wish you'd let me send it to your home."

"I don't want it. I wouldn't read it. When you didn't call for all of June, it was hard on me. I felt left behind. I got drunk one night. I smashed your flute. I smashed it against the bathroom sink. I did it poorly, though. I wound up needing stitches."

"You . . . smashed the flute?"

He could hear the utter heartbreak in her voice at the thought of it. He wished he hadn't said it. He looked at his hand where the scar sat like a constellation across his palm.

"I couldn't play anymore. It was too painful."

"I understand. I was in a bad place when I last saw you. I'm not fully out of it. It's gonna take me a lot of time and work. I've had to realize just how weak I am. But I need you to know, Rashid, I need you to know my love for you was real. It was real, and if we had met under different circumstances . . ."

"I get it. Everything could have been different."

"I'd like to think so. Don't you?"

He saw the rats scurrying, danger was imminent.

"The train is coming, Rachel. I have to go."

"The train is coming. How poetic. I loved you, Rashid, and you loved me. Let's never doubt that, okay?"

"Agreed."

"Last chance for you to give me your address. If not, I'll just burn this letter."

The train pulled into the station and cut them off. It was the last time he would ever hear her voice.

One afternoon he sat outside Comforti's in the glorious autumn sun, eating a chunk of garlic bread and smoking a cigarette. The afternoon crowd had thinned out, and he had left the last two tables to the new guy, an actor from Philadelphia. Lucia had asked him to take a walk with her, and he wondered what was on her mind. The last time they had taken a walk was a little over a year ago, when she had broken the news that she was giving him a two-dollar raise and moving him to the position of head waiter. He watched through the windows of the restaurant as she transitioned from the bar to the cash register to the hostess, and eventually emerged from the place, putting her hair back in a ponytail. He stamped out his cigarette as she took him by the arm.

"You and this smoking. Quit, don't quit. Quit, don't quit."

"I'm pretty horrible, aren't I?"

"Only you can know why you do these things. We walk."

The sidewalk was bustling with locals as they moved at a smooth and steady pace.

"Don't you just love this kind of day when everybody in the city seems to have a renewed spirit and energy about them?" she said.

"It's the kind of day that makes New Yorkers shine."

"It's true, love. It's true. So, listen, I have to go to Sicily next week."

"Really? That's sudden, no?"

"Yes, it is always like this. Sudden and urgent. My aunt Rosalie, she has been diagnosed with the final stage breast cancer. She doesn't have long."

"Rosalie. She's the one who has never come to the States."

"Right, she is afraid to fly. Never left home really, poor thing. Anyway, I must pay my respects."

"I'm sorry, Mrs. C. Were the two of you close?"

"Not at all, but still my mother adores her so I will go and support. Life, it is always random, you know? Everything, it is just random. But listen, while I am away, I know something. You know Mario and his new restaurant? It is going very well and I imagine it will be quite successful, knowing his skills and that area's population. Very soon he is going to approach you, and it will be to steal you from me, but to work in the kitchen, not as a waiter. You have shown tremendous skill in the kitchen, sweetheart. It has not gone unnoticed. He will come to you with an offer."

"Don't worry, Mrs. C, I won't leave you guys."

"Like hell you will not. You will accept this offer, Rashid. It will be a great opportunity for you."

He looked to her, somewhat surprised.

"I don't understand. You want me to go?"

"What I want is what any mother wants for her son, which is to say, I want what is best for you. There is no way I expect you to wait tables all of your life, no way. You don't want that, do you? Please tell me you don't want that for yourself."

"What I really don't want is to let you down."

"Let me down? This is not possible for you, sweetheart. I should say the only way you can do this is by not living up to your true level of where you need to be. How do they say? Your potential."

"Have I done something wrong, Mrs. C?"

They stopped walking, and she turned to face him head on. It was always his opinion that no white woman that he knew personally had ever aged more beautifully than Lucia Comforti. She had soft brown eyes that stood out vividly on her lightly wrinkled, soft pink face. He scanned those eyes and saw nothing but affection in them. She was holding his face in her hands.

"Rashid, you have outgrown this place. When you first came to us you were still very much young, very much searching for a place to fit. You needed us and we needed you. But now, you are still young, but you are so much wiser. So much more mature. It is your time to move forward and take more chances. Mario is going to provide you with this chance. It may be scary, but you must embrace it. We will always be here for you. You will always be a Comforti. But someday, Antony and I want to come dine at your restaurant. We want to be your first customers. For this to happen, you must move forward. Tell me you understand."

He took her hand in his and he kissed it. He knew that what she had stated was true. When he had first come to work there, he'd had no compass. They had offered him the opportunity to move from one restaurant to another, and he'd taken it, basically for the change of scenery. He'd had no idea what he wanted from life, and he hadn't been interested in the question. He'd had no desire to ponder his future. He had just wanted to be somewhere. But he had come to realize that just being somewhere wasn't enough anymore. No admirable person just accepted mediocrity.

"I just, uh, I just can't imagine a life without you guys."

"And you don't have to. We are not going anywhere."

Less than two weeks later, he was sitting at the bar at Comforti's at the end of the evening when Antony handed him the phone. It was Mario on the other end, asking him to meet up later on that week at a popular bar across the street from Yankee Stadium. When he agreed to the date, Antony winked at him.

The bar was packed with fans watching the Yankees square off against the Boston Red Sox in the American League playoffs. The fact that they were playing Boston stung just a little, as it forced him to think of her, not that he needed to be forced at this point. He still reflected on her daily. He found Mario at a table in the rear, wearing a Yankees jersey, eating from a huge plate of calamari, and drinking from a pitcher of Budweiser. The two hugged, ate, and drank a lot. Somewhere around the fifth inning, Mario got down to it.

"Listen, no more beating around the bush, okay? We both know why I invited you here. It's no secret."

"Humor me, Mario. Just a little."

"Lucia and Antony have already given me their blessing. You know my new place in Park Slope will be open in December. I want you to be a part of my team in the kitchen."

"Whoa, whoa—you want a *mulignan* in your kitchen?"

"I have a *mulignan* in my bed every night, why not in my kitchen too?"

They talked well into the night, Mario presenting his vision for the restaurant and assuring him that as long as their doors were open, he would always have a place there. He had to admit, he was both intrigued by the new opportunity and flattered to be wanted. As he had promised Lucia, he accepted the role, and they went their separate ways around midnight, both stumbling drunk to their individual train platforms. He finally had the feeling that his life was progressing.

He spent one last Christmas season at Comforti's before starting up at Mario's new place, Amalfi Sunset. He stayed on mainly to train his replacement, an enthusiastic and annoyingly perky Puerto Rican woman named Sonia. Truth be told, Sonia should not have survived long at the job. She was terrible with numbers, often calculated the closing till incorrectly, and screwed up orders on a regular basis, giving people at the table the wrong plates, causing them to have to shuffle them around once she had left. A few customers complained that she talked too much and overshared parts of her life with them, and Lucia pulled him aside one day to ask his advice, as she had half a mind to fire Sonia before the Thanksgiving rush. He would have agreed, but Sonia had one huge ace up her sleeve: Sonia was the single mom of everyone's favorite seven-year-old kid, Osman, who often came in with her at the beginning of her shift, and charmed all who met him.

Osman was truly the only reason Sonia was able to stay on at the job, so strong was the crew's affection for him. Nobody wanted to see the kid go. After some discussion, Rashid assured Lucia that even if he had to work with her seven days a week, he would get Sonia up and running to at least a competent level by Christmas. As she always had, Lucia believed in him. It took a while, but by early December, Sonia was deemed adequate enough to stay on as his replacement.

He and the kid had developed a pattern—whenever the two arrived for her shift, while Sonia got into her outfit downstairs, he and the kid would sit at the bar. Over coffee and hot chocolate with marshmallows, they would go over football news and make picks on all the upcoming games that Sunday before the sitter came and picked him up for the day. After a few weeks, Antony and a few other crew members joined in the morning gathering, as Osman proved to be a better picker than all of them, and they were making quite a little profit placing bets on his choices with Antony's bookie in Syosset.

One afternoon Sonia approached Rashid at the end of the lunch rush; she seemed even more anxious than her normal self. She had met a man on the subway a couple of weeks ago, a "Wall Street type" as she put it, and after several dates, he wanted to take her away for a weekend to his house in Montauk. She wanted to go, but her mother had just come out of back surgery, her sister was out of town, and she had no one to take care of Osman all weekend. It would be a Friday morning to Sunday night commitment, and she begged him to consider, even offered to pay him. He swiped away at that offer and, after conferring with his mother, agreed to take the kid in. Sonia was beside herself with relief and pledged to make it up to him someday.

That Friday Osman stayed at the restaurant all day, mostly reading at a side table, and at the end of his shift, Rashid took the kid out to see a Disney movie playing at the local cinema. On the subway ride home, Osman fell asleep in his arms and Rashid had to carry him to his apartment. When he got there, Rashid's mother helped him take his shoes off and they placed him in Rashid's bed. Rashid slept on the couch all weekend.

In the morning, his mother made breakfast for all of them, and then he and Osman took off for the Bronx Zoo, where they spent the afternoon. Osman waited at a table while Rashid got in line at the zoo's café to order lunch for the two of them. A woman with a familiar face approached him. She was wearing a Fordham sweatsuit.

"Hey, you waited on me once," she said.

"Did I?"

"Yeah, the Italian place over off Arthur Avenue."

"Comforti's."

"Yeah, it was great. I was there with some of my homegirls."

"Oh yeah, I think that was last summer, was it?"

"Right, right, my birthday. I, uh, I think I got a little drunk and left you my number."

"Ah, right. I was in a crazy spot at that time."

"No need for excuses. It's all good. Bernadette."

"Rashid."

They shook hands; she had a strong handshake, stronger than his.

"Nice. So, what are you up to today, Rashid?"

"Well, I'm taking care of my coworker's son all weekend, while she's away. That's him over there."

"Nice, cute guy."

"Yeah, he's alright. What are you up to?"

"Well, I was actually just taking a break from my studies. Needed to get my face out of the books, you know? Figured I'd walk down and check out some of those Siberian tigers I heard so much about."

"Yeah, they weren't too open to socializing when we passed by."

"Yeah, right? That kinda seems to be the thing this afternoon. It's like all the animals were out partying last night or something."

"We were saying the same thing."

He looked at her, looked around her, and realized she was alone. On some level he was surprised that such an attractive woman would be out just wandering around the zoo on her own on a Saturday afternoon.

"Hey, do you want to join me and Osman for a little lunch?"

"Oh, are you sure? That would be great. It's kinda lonely out here."

The three had a pleasant lunch over chicken strips and fries, and Bernadette wound up spending the next two hours walking around the zoo with them. Though most of the animals remained out of sight for the day, they still managed to have some laughs and enjoy themselves. Bernadette laughed freely and fit smoothly into their routine. It was as if they had known her for days, not hours. When it was all over and they walked through the exit doors, she turned to thank them for the day.

"We're gonna go roller skating now. Maybe you can come with us?" Osman offered up.

Rashid looked at the kid and back to her. There was an awkward silence as the idea wafted over them. Bernadette looked at him with a look that said, "I'm game if you're game."

"We were gonna go grab a quick bite at the restaurant," he said. "Then we're gonna head over to Staten Island. You wanna come to Comforti's?"

"How about this? How about I go back to the dorm, shower quickly, then meet you guys over at Comforti's?"

"Sounds good."

"Sounds great!" Osman added.

At Comforti's they snacked on pizza bites and drank hot chocolate at the bar. They were reviewing tomorrow's football picks together when Bernadette entered and joined them. Rashid was immediately taken with how lovely she looked. She was wearing skinny jeans, a cashmere blue sweater. She had managed to borrow her roommate's car for the night, which meant they wouldn't have to take the subway at all.

At the end of the meal, the three of them piled into the Honda Civic, and they spent a fun evening at the roller rink. Turned out, she was raised in Phoenix, Arizona. She was adopted as a baby by a white family and raised with two white sisters and one Vietnamese sister. She had been attending Fordham on a basketball scholarship, but a serious injury her freshman year put an end to all that, and she was now pursuing a career in education with the hope of teaching in the public-school system someday.

At one point Rashid had grown tired of skating in circles, and he opted to hang out in the lounge for a bit and leave the two of them to it. He sat in the lounge, drank a bottle of root beer, and watched the two as Bernadette knelt down and tied the kid's skate for him. Somewhere in this gem of a moment, it occurred to him that someday he might not mind having a child of his own.

At the end of the night, Bernadette was insistent on driving them home, but he—out of fear and shame, not wanting her to experience his neighborhood—insisted that she drive herself home and that they would catch the subway. With Osman asleep in his arms, Rashid walked her to the car. After getting out the keys, she turned to him.

"Hey, I don't think you know how great this day was for me. I needed it."

"We had a good time, yes?"

"Yes, and I'm gonna miss this guy. You think we can do it again sometime soon?"

"Yeah, yeah, sure. I'll talk to Osman's mom next week and see what we can come up with."

"Great. You know, you can call me too if you want. Just some adult time could be nice too."

"I hear you, that would be nice. Like I told you, I'll be starting that new position soon, but I'm sure once I get settled in and everything, I'll have a lot more time for all the fun stuff."

"Good, great. It'll be a bummer not to have you in the neighborhood anymore."

"I'll be back from time to time. The Comfortis are my family."

"Well, I'll wait to hear from you, then."

"Yeah, take care of yourself."

"Take care of this guy."

She kissed sleeping Osman's forehead, then leaned in towards Rashid and the two had one of those prickly moments where she went to kiss his cheek and he went to kiss her other cheek and faces bashed uncomfortably. They said good night with a handshake, and he watched her drive off.

Eighteen

He started at Amalfi Sunset on January 2, and the workload was exhausting. The place was situated right on the corner of a very popular intersection of a thriving neighborhood, and was night and day from Comforti's. Rashid's former job had the intimacy of a small bedroom. The new place was more like a large pool hall. Customers came in by the dozens, all throughout the day. He had never imagined so many people could afford to eat out so regularly. At first it produced a little anxiety within him, but once he got into a rhythm, he started to settle in.

The night of his first shift, his mother came in with Stacie and two of their aunts. They were all dressed up as if they were attending a lavish affair, and they fawned over him when he came to the table to greet them. He blushed as he introduced them to several of his colleagues, and after they had finished dessert, they commended Rashid and Mario on one of the greatest meals they had ever eaten. He felt a slight tug of pride in his chest as he watched his mother get emotional while thanking Mario for giving her son the opportunity. His boss played it off as if he were the one who should be thankful, then sent two complimentary bottles of wine over to their table. After his shift was over, Rashid drank with them in his sweaty chef's outfit.

Later that week Marlon came in with Stefani, beaming with the news that they were pregnant. They celebrated with a bottle of champagne, and he treated them to dinner. On the subway ride home, he and Marlon debated baby names while Stefani slept on his shoulder. The image of her was enough to remind him of the time that Rachel had done the same—fallen asleep on his shoulder after a night out. He could still see the strap of her white dress dangling off her left shoulder and remember how strong and whole it made him feel to pull it back up for her.

In his heart, he was comfortable with himself. He knew that he had overcome the bulk of the malaise of losing her, but there were still many days when he wished she were a part of him. At times, these moments caught him off guard, like while chopping onions, or while picking up muffins from a bakery, or sipping coffee by the balcony window of the second floor of the restaurant. One day, he entered Mario's office and found his business partner, Gretchen, working at the computer while listening to the live production of an opera. He took in the orchestrations for a few moments before recognizing the leitmotif from *Tosca*.

"Are you okay?" Gretchen, a full-bodied woman with a slight German accent and a brilliant head of dyed-purple hair, asked him. "You look like you are about to cry."

"Must be all that Puccini," he half joked.

He wanted Rachel to see how much his life had improved. He wanted to assure her, "See, I told you I wouldn't be a waiter forever." He wanted her to know that there were days when he dreamed of opening his own restaurant, and that when he did, he would buy one of her mother's sculptures and feature it prominently at the restaurant's entrance. He might even name the restaurant Pagliacci, if he went with an Italian place. Eventually he realized that what he still desired more than nearly anything else was to impress Rachel. He wanted her to know without a scintilla of doubt that he deserved to be in her life, that he wasn't just an appendage, a pleasant distraction. He wanted to hear her acknowledge that he mattered. Some days it saddened him more than he cared to admit. One day he opened his phone and pulled her phone number up. His finger hovered over the dial button for close to a minute before he closed it.

He started keeping a consistent Sunday afternoon date with Osman. He would pick the kid up from Sonia's place around noon, and they would usually catch a movie or just have a bite to eat. Sometimes they ate at Comforti's, which gave him the opportunity to catch up with his old crew. For Super Bowl Sunday, Bernadette invited them to the campus, and they watched the event with a bunch of students in a recreation hall. Something had changed about his relationship with Bernadette since she had returned from her holiday break in Arizona. She seemed less interested in a romantic entanglement, and he was actually fine with that. Since he spent so much time at work, he didn't really have time to think about anything deep or time consuming.

Rashid developed a friendship with two of his colleagues in the kitchen. One, a middle-aged Italian guy named Vic, who once owned a gay bar in Queens, and who had known Mario since they were teenagers, and the other, a Greek guy in his early twenties who they all called Rocky due to his uncanny resemblance to the fictional movie character. Vic and Rocky shared a three-bedroom apartment in Bensonhurst that Vic's uncle once owned, and Rashid spent so many nights a week there drinking after work, by the end of March, they all decided it would be best if he just moved in. His mother was sad to see him go, but at the same time, she was relieved. She had started dating a Dominican guy who ran his own private-cab company and things were heating up between them.

Bernadette came by his new apartment one rainy afternoon with a gift—a fancy new desk lamp. She had come over rather unexpectedly, and she had caught him in the midst of hurriedly dressing for work. He could tell right away that something was off with her—there was something on her mind—but he didn't know just how to bring it up. She asked if she could walk with him to work. On the way, they talked about school and her upcoming exams, and when they got to the restaurant, he offered to treat her to lunch. She turned him down, claiming she had to get back to her studies, and bolted out of the place, leaving him somewhat confused.

Later that night at the end of his shift, he answered a phone call from her. It was just past midnight and she had never called him that late before. He could hear an anxiety in her voice.

"Hey, how are you?"

"I'm okay, busy night here tonight. What's up with you? You never call this late."

"I know. I—"

She was crying.

"Hey, Bernie, what's going on? Talk to me."

"Are you off soon? Can I see you?"

He met her at a bar called the Outfield, two blocks away from her dorm. It was full of college students out on a Friday night and a few locals. He found her sitting at a table near the jukebox. She was wearing a denim skirt and a flannel shirt. She looked like she hadn't slept in a while. He brought them each a beer and a scotch and just sat and listened to her. She had a lot to get off her chest. A couple of years back, she had needed to see a doctor to undergo a certain procedure, a "female thing of a very sensitive nature." The procedure went fine, but she would have to be tested on a regular basis and there was the slight possibility that she could someday develop cervical cancer. This embarrassed her, and it made intimacy awkward and, at times, uncomfortable. Though many of her friends at school were regularly "getting busy," she refrained. She hadn't had sex in two years. The thought of it scared her.

"I'm so sorry, Bernie. Is there anything I can do?"

"That's the worst part. I never imagined . . . this is not what I wanted . . . for us."

"What do you mean? What did you want for us?"

The way she looked at him, it was the way he imagined a genius must look at a complete imbecile who can't add two and two and get four.

"Rashid, when I left for the holiday, I could barely think of anything but . . ."

He watched her eyes, and he knew what she meant all at once. It hadn't occurred to him; he had been so caught up in his own world. Now, with Led Zeppelin blaring in this room that reeked of beer, body odor, and marijuana, he could see that his life could be changing soon. Somewhere, in a deep chamber, a candle was being relit.

He took on more responsibilities at the restaurant. He started doing a lot more of the ordering of food and supplies. It put him in touch with an entire new industry of manufacturers and laborers. Sometimes he was sent in person to examine and evaluate the merchandise. He liked these days "out in the field," a nice break from the humdrum and rigmarole of the kitchen. Mario was the type of person who didn't offer up praise and commendation easily. He felt that young people were too reliant on it. It made a lot of staffers uncomfortable, not knowing where they stood with the boss, but Rashid took it all in stride. He was confident, and he was grateful. He knew that every time Mario gave him a new task, it meant Mario believed in him more. He assisted with formulating the scheduling of the kitchen staff, which meant a lot of his coworkers started sucking up to him to get favored schedules. He'd come in and find a nice cigar in his workspace, or a decent bottle of sherry.

One evening Lucia and Antony came by with a bottle of wine for him. He didn't often serve customers, but he shooed aside their assigned waiter and insisted on dutifully waiting on them himself. He brought out every portion of their meal, from the opening glass of water to the final crème brûlée. With each appearance Lucia rose to meet him and he kissed her hand. Seeing their pride for him was overwhelming, and he had to excuse himself for a moment to go out back, where he smoked a cigarette through tears. When he returned, Lucia and Antony were gone. He, of course, had intended to treat them to their meal, but not only had they paid in cash, leaving an enormous tip behind, they'd also left behind a tiny envelope with his name on it. When he opened the envelope, he found two tickets to this Saturday's matinee performance of *La Bohème* and a little note: *Don't worry, son, we already cleared it with Mario. You have this Saturday off. Take that pretty young student you keep bringing around . . . A and L.*

As he stood on the balcony of the Metropolitan Opera House in his gray suit, he remembered how awkward he had felt that first time with Rachel. How the opera crowd had left him feeling like an interloper, an impostor, a deadly virus that slipped into the castle late at night.

Just why he felt more like he belonged this time around was somewhat of an enigma to him. He had pondered it as he tried to put himself in Bernadette's place. Bernadette had been raised by white people, grown up in their Hallmark card settings. The odds were much greater that she had been to, or was even familiar with, the opera more than any other Black people he ever knew.

But still, he wondered what had changed to make him so much more comfortable with the thought of entering this world again. Maybe it was the subtle things. Like when he first attended *Tosca* with Rachel and he went to go use the restroom. He had shared the sink bay with a white guy in a suit, and the guy had said to him, "Your lady drag you along too? Honestly, I'd rather be at the Yankees game." The guy had handed him a few paper towels on the way out and then left. It was a simple interaction, but it stayed with him, and when he returned to his seat, he reflected on it as the next act began. Was it possible that two things could be true at the same time? That he and that white guy in the suit were very different and yet they were not so different? Or was it the fact that he had slowly been discovering more about the inner lives of white privilege and what he saw there did not overly impress him? He had always held the notion that he could easily live in their world, but most of them could never live in his. Experience plus confidence had given him the slightest feeling of superiority these past couple of years. He felt like they should be grateful to have his presence at the opera. His presence reminded them that they still had work to do. He saw himself as a humbler and an equalizer.

For a long time Rashid had been afraid of what Rachel brought to his life. The idea hit him, after months of reflection, that love had been terrifying to him. Love trotted out a chorus line of your worst fears and encouraged them to dance on your chest. It caused you to doubt yourself in ways detrimental and extremely irrational. Love came at a price: it asked you to wear your skin inside out, exposing your veins to the public at large.

He had done a lot of reading on the subject. Animals loved each other, but with animals it was a little different. Animals, like humans, came together out of necessity. There was the all-encompassing need to procreate—to protect the species. Animals often came together to ward off predators. With humans, the predators were already inside us. Humans created their own demons and sought emotional safety from others in an effort to fight those demons. He made a promise to himself—whoever came along after Rachel, he would give them a stronger chance than he had originally given himself. He would make a concerted effort to drown out the voices of doubt that would attempt to shade him from vulnerability.

He watched Bernadette emerge from the bathroom, looking like royalty in a red evening gown. She had even worn a tiara. He liked that about her—she had a playful nature that was infectious. He offered his arm to her, which she took graciously, and together they walked up the steps back to the mezzanine. He enjoyed seeing the excitement on her face at the pageantry of it all. She was anxious to return to their seats and start act 2; to learn what fate had in store for all the poor, sick, downtrodden characters. As it turned out, this was indeed her first opera, and he was honored to bring it to her, just as someone else had done for him.

Later that night in her dorm room, under a full moon that hung in the sky like a bright bowl of milk, they moved without and within one another on the upper level of her bunk bed. Damp fingers gripped at shoulders and biceps. Warm mouths relieved pressure. He had to be careful with her; she was figuring out all over again just what brought her pleasure and what was uncomfortable. He did his best to listen and respond. He discovered, to his wonder, that he was able to give himself fully to her, to completely focus on pleasing and being pleased. He had expected to be haunted by ghosts of Rachel's passion, and to his relief, that was not the case when he was with Bernadette. For the first time in a long time, he felt whole again. It was not dissimilar to surviving a deadly illness.

One terribly humid afternoon in July, Mario had him make a field run to a kitchenware supplier in downtown Manhattan. At first, Rashid was not pleased about the assignment. The subway was the most unpleasant place in the city to be on a day like that, but he quickly realized that the address of the supplier was just two blocks away from a location that he had oftentimes wanted to visit, but never could work up the nerve to do so. As he walked out of the Prince Street subway station, he turned and headed east. His appointment with the supplier wasn't for another ninety minutes or so. He recognized the gallery right away, although everything about its appearance had changed. When he walked in he saw the host, a tall, skinny man wearing a silver jumpsuit and high heels.

The host was speaking to someone who looked like a repairman, so he wandered around on his own, taking in a series of paintings on the wall. He did not know the names of any of the artists, and after a couple of minutes, he found himself bored and began to question why he'd come there in the first place. The host eventually came up to him. He had soft hazel eyes and the grace of a ballerina.

"Well, hello, young fella. Is there anything I can tell you about any of these works?"

"Honestly, no. I was just curious."

"Are you an artist yourself?"

"Me, no. But I was in here, like, over a year ago, and there was an artist I really liked, Muriel Auslander."

"Oh, Muriel Auslander, yes, she is divine. I've always had an affection for her work. She hasn't got anything coming up that I know of, and that isn't surprising. You know she had a stroke, right?"

"No, did she? I didn't know."

"Yeah, last I heard, she was pretty much out of it. Poor thing probably won't ever create again. At least not in the corporeal sense. There is an artist over here who I would say has a similar aesthetic to a Muriel Auslander. He's Cuban, straight out of Havana. Can I show you some of his work?"

"That's okay. I really just wanted to browse."

"You browse away, honey. Let me know if you want some coffee."

As he watched the host walk away, he put his hand to his forehead and thought about how agonizing that must feel for an artist to lose the ability to create. He wanted to go to her, to visit the old lady, to hold her hand. But he wasn't sure it was appropriate, and in the end he decided against it. Rashid did however make one other trip. He hopped in a taxi and went straight over to the jazz club where the brother played. He walked into the room and saw a trio of young Black guys warming up onstage. A bartender let him know they wouldn't be open for business for a few hours. He asked the man for a schedule of upcoming bands and was disappointed to see that the brother wasn't scheduled to play there until late in the fall. In the taxi ride back to his appointment, he made a decision to do something he hadn't done in years—he would write a letter.

That night, after the work shift had ended, he sat at a table way in the back of the restaurant with a glass of scotch and ice, wearing his stained chef's outfit. He had two pieces of restaurant stationery with him and a pen. After burying his head in his hand for a moment, he took a swig and started to write while waitstaff cleared tables all around him. He had thought he knew exactly what he wanted to say— he wanted Muriel to know that he had heard about her condition and that she was in his thoughts—but as he started to write, he realized he had no idea what he was doing.

Dear Muriel,

It has been a while, huh? I bet you never expected to get a letter from me. Hell, I haven't written a letter since I was a little kid in summer camp and I wrote to my mom begging her to come get me. It was my first time away from home and I felt afraid. I hate feeling afraid. I never want to let fear rule me. And yet, it does at times. I am working on it, I really am. But it isn't easy, you know? I wonder if you ever deal with fear. You have always seemed like such a strong person to me, and I could never imagine you letting something like fear control your life. But I do remember Rachel once told me that you never take the subway. She said that you were probably afraid of subways and trains because they reminded you of something awful. Of childhood trauma. She said you would probably never forget that train ride you took from your ghetto in Poland to that concentration camp. I forget the name now. I know it was a deeply traumatic time for you. It was where you lost much of your family.

Rachel told me a lot about you, and to tell you the truth, I learned a lot about myself from the both of you.

It's strange for me to say this to you now, and it will probably be stranger for you to hear it, but I think you should know: I loved Rachel once. Loved her with all of my heart. I still do in a way. And I think, I'm pretty sure, that she loved me deeply as well. I don't know what her life is like today, but I'm sure that wherever she is, she is happy and moving forward. I hope that she thinks about me every now and then, and I hope that when she does, she thinks of me fondly, like I think of the two of you. I'm so thankful that I met you both at Comforti's. It has made all the difference in my life.

He stared down at that last sentence for what seemed to him a very long time. Something felt wrong to him; something felt off. He scanned the letter and the word "fear" leapt out at him. He took a last swig, tossed the glass aside, and crumpled the letter violently. He walked outside, borrowed a cigarette from one of his colleagues, and lit it. He didn't smoke the cigarette but used it instead to light the crumpled letter on fire. He watched it burn in his hand, and he let the searing heat touch the flesh of his palm until he could no longer take the pain. As he tossed away the ashes, a thought occurred to him: he wanted to go visit his brother.

He had to switch work shifts with Vic in order to go see Darnell. Rikers had a strict schedule in which inmates whose last name began with *A* through *L* could only be visited Wednesdays and Saturdays, and there were no visitors allowed on Sundays and Mondays, his normal days off. He chose to go on the Wednesday in September right before Labor Day. He couldn't sleep the entire night before. His mother was the only one who actually approved of his visit.

"You know that nigga is a sociopath, right?" was how Marlon put it.

"I get why you might want to do this, but I honestly can't imagine any good coming of it. Your mom can't see it, but Darnell has always been an unethical piece of shit," was how Stacie put it.

Why did he want to do it? This was a question that still clung to him like a cobweb, even as he deboarded the bus from Downtown Brooklyn and stood before the massive prison. What did he hope to gain? His memory of the last time he physically saw his brother was still fresh in his mind. His mother had begged him to go to the courthouse with her to be there for his sentencing. The courtroom was loaded with brown people on both sides of the issue. When the judge said "Life," Darnell turned to him and his mother and smiled while holding up a peace sign. His front tooth had been knocked out in some recent altercation, and he was wearing his hair in pigtails that made him appear cartoonish and demented. His mother had cried. Rashid had just felt relief. He knew if he never saw his brother again, he could go on just fine. It would probably be healthier for him. That was nearly a decade ago.

On the bus ride up, he had sat next to a plain-looking Black woman around his age who dressed like a preacher's wife. They had struck up a conversation about their visits. She was going to see her fiancé, who was in for aggravated assault on his stepfather. She had only communicated with the man through letters, and this would be her first time ever seeing him in the flesh.

"What if he's not as good-looking as you imagined?" he had asked her half-jokingly.

"We talk on the phone, and his letters show me where his heart is. He's a real poet. A romantic. That's all I'm looking for. Good-looking often leads to trouble."

It was so odd to Rashid, the notion that you could fall for someone without touch, without eyes, without a tongue tasting the inside of a thigh, without a nose smelling a neck. But then again, he got it. Love was like that. It didn't often make absolute sense. In fact, it could be downright unreasonable. Now, he and the woman were parting, heading for different sections. He put his hand on her shoulder.

"Good luck with your man," he said.

"Don't need luck. I have the Lord," she replied.

The waiting room was sterile and uninviting. He sat at a tiny table with a phone receiver in the center of a glass partition. It was just like his mother described it. It was just like you saw on cop shows. The woman next to him was crying to a prisoner on the other side about how their uncle still beat her, beat her even more now that the man was gone. He couldn't hear the man's response. After a few minutes of sitting there, a door on the other side of the glass swung open and his older brother swaggered in, wearing a blue jumpsuit and grinning that grin that only the most arrogant men can. When their eyes connected, he realized it had all been a bad idea. He had nothing in common with the man sitting before him. He never had. His brother took a few seconds to pick up his receiver, milking the stare down.

"Well, well, the prodigal nigga returns."

"How you doing, Darnell?"

"How I'm doing? That's your question for me? I'm doing great, man. Life is just super. How are you, little man?"

"You know, getting by."

"Ma tells me you all running shit in the kitchen. She say you on some real Julia Child shit."

"Julia . . ."

"Forget it, man. Clearly you don't watch much TV."

Rashid nodded, amazed by the fact that all of a sudden he felt like a teenaged boy again.

"So, what's up, nigga? What brings you by? You need to borrow some money?"

"Money? No."

"I know. I was just joking with you. What that gonna look like—you coming to me to borrow money? Shit."

"You look healthy."

"Ain't no man ever got fat off prison food, I tell you that right now. Ain't got much to do up in this bitch but watch TV, work out, and jerk off. Speaking of, I hear you got a girlfriend, college girl."

"Ma tells you a lot."

"Man, what you come by for?"

"I wanted to see how you were doing."

"Oh, what, after all these years you wanna see how a nigga doing?"

"I don't know. You was on my mind lately."

"What was you thinking about? All those times I whipped your ass? I know you still got that scar from when I stabbed yo ass with that screwdriver. I bet you never wear another man's clothes again after that!"

He felt a familiar heat forming at the base of his forehead. He remembered a room on fire.

"I was thinking about a lot."

"Oh yeah? Tell me. What was you thinking about?"

"I was thinking . . . I was thinking of the fire, when we were kids. I was thinking of how, you know, I was careless. And that carelessness may have had a negative effect on you."

"Carelessness?"

He watched his brother's face. The grin had faded by now, replaced by a chiseled animosity. He seemed to be chewing the word "carelessness" the way a coyote chews on the leg of a goat.

"Carelessness? Nigga, what you know about carelessness? You wasn't careless. You was just stupid. And your stupidity caused me to lose more than half my skin. But I ain't trying to worry about that, 'cause you didn't do shit that didn't make me stronger. You didn't do a damn thing to me I couldn't handle. Shit, what you think, huh? You think in some way you hurt me or something?"

"I was just saying."

"You was just saying nothing! Listen to me, little man. I don't need your scrawny Black ass coming up here to see me, talking some regrets.

You don't know shit about regrets. You know what I regret? I shoulda killed yo ass back then. Shoulda killed you twice. But I held back. I held back because I knew you was a pussy-ass mama's boy and the last thing I wanted was to see our mama suffer losing you. That was the last shit I needed."

"I don't understand."

"You don't understand what?"

"I don't understand, then, your hostility. Why you always treated me that way."

"Oh, what? What's the matter, you gonna cry now? What's the matter, Shid, you was the victim? Did I terrorize your pussy ass?"

The words rang true, and before he knew what to make of them, hot tears were dotting his cold cheeks.

"I never meant to hurt you."

"What did you say? Nigga, have you been listening to anything I said? You *can't* hurt me, Shid. Dudes like you are not capable of hurting dudes like me. You are a fucking simpleton. You a pawn on the chessboard. I'm a knight moving my way towards king, you hear me? I'm surprised you got a woman. Is that it? You shoulda heard how me and my boys talked about you behind your back. You know who liked sucking this dick? Your favorite cousin, Stacie. That's who liked sucking this dick. Ask her about it."

Rashid hung up the phone and rose from his seat. His brother was still talking, flailing dramatically with his arms now, grabbing savagely at his crotch at one point. He wiped his face, looked around him, and walked out into a rainy afternoon. While waiting for the bus, he called Stacie. She was at her internship working at an off-Broadway theatre when she picked up.

"Hey, how'd it go?"

"It was terrible. Can I see you?"

They met at a cozy martini bar on Forty-Second Street, with dark lighting that cast everyone in a shadowy blue tint. He told her everything about the visit, and when he became emotional, she held him close and stroked his neck. He took the last part slowly, carefully, concerned about how she would process it all. He had to know what Darnell had meant. It was gnawing at his head from inside. He told her exactly what his brother had said, word for word. He watched her intently.

"We don't have to talk about that," she said.

"You can tell me, Stacie. Did you and Darnell . . ."

"Please," she said, standing up. He watched her sit down and stand up again. "Can we get a smoke?"

They stood under the awning of the bar. For a minute or so, they just smoked and watched the traffic gleaming in the rain. When she spoke, it was even paced, devoid of emotion.

"Remember those weekends I used to crash with you guys? It was one of those nights when you fell asleep early, and your mom was out clubbing with her girls, and it was just me and Darnell watching cable in the living room. He had been smoking weed, may have been crack, even. He . . . made me do some things. He forced himself on me. He made me do some things that to this day I still can't fully shake. But the past is the past, you know?" He watched her, fascinated by how calm and stoic she was. He envied her, but felt just the opposite. A rage boiled within.

"That motherfucker. I'll fucking kill him."

"No, no. Listen to me, Shid. No. That right there is part of the problem. That is the pattern we need to stop. That response needs to end. Don't ever tell your mother any of this, you hear me? Ever."

"Why not? Why shouldn't she know about this? She been treating this nigga like he some type of wounded animal. She needs to know the truth about him."

"I understand where you are coming from, but listen to me—I've come to realize that the truth, it can be overrated. It's not always helpful. Sometimes we're just better off not knowing things."

"That's why you went to Florida, isn't it?"

"It was for the best. I couldn't be here with him so close."

"Marlon was right."

"'Marlon was right'? That's not a phrase I hear often." She shook his shoulder playfully and the two stood there quietly, finishing off their cigarettes. "It's funny, all that talk I do about the horrors of the white man. And don't get me wrong, it's valid. But a lot of times, especially for us, the person who murders you is often someone who looks just like you."

He put a lot more of his lifeblood into the restaurant, into his craft. With Mario's financial assistance, he took classes two nights a week at a school in Queens and he expanded his culinary talents. He started with a few Greek dishes, spanakopita, souvlaki, baked eggplant with feta. On Christmas Eve, he made youvetsi, beef stew with orzo, for Sonia, Osman, and Bernadette, at Sonia's place. The meal was a huge hit, and after putting Osman to bed, Rashid sat at the table with Sonia and Bernadette. Sonia had asked them to stay behind for a while.

Over herbal tea and vanilla wafers, he listened as Sonia, with moisture in her eyes, relayed that she had recently found a small bump in her breast, and though the doctors let her know it wasn't actually serious, a false positive, it got her to thinking. Osman would never know his father. She needed to know someone would be there for Osman if something happened to her, and Rashid was the only man she truly trusted. She asked him to be Osman's godfather, and he accepted the title instantly.

For Osman's birthday that March, he and Bernadette took him to see the matinee performance of a Broadway show that was based on a hugely successful animated television character. After the show, they met up with Stacie, who had gotten them the tickets through her theatre connections. They all ate at a huge tourist trap of a restaurant in

Times Square. When Bernadette took Osman to the bathroom, Stacie yanked his ear.

"Why you keep this great girl hidden all this time?"

"I didn't keep her hidden. You're very busy, I'm very busy, she's very busy. It's hard to get schedules together."

"Man, you been holding out."

"Why would I hold out?"

"You tell me? You gonna marry the woman or what?"

"Whoa, whoa, slow it down, girl! Slow it down. I haven't even met her parents yet."

"You ain't met the parents yet? What the hell you waiting for?"

"Well, I told you they live in Arizona."

"Nigga, they got these things called planes."

"I'm not comfortable with them. Anyway, I told you she was adopted, right? There's a little more—her parents are white."

He watched as Stacie's expression changed from amused to slightly bewildered.

"Oooooooh. She on some of that *Diff'rent Strokes* shit. Interesting."

"Yeah. I was a little hesitant about you meeting her."

"Wait, what? You thought because she had some white parents, I was gonna hold that against her?"

"I didn't know, Stacie. I wasn't sure."

"Jesus, Rashid. I thought I made this clear to you long ago. I don't hate white people, okay? I live in New Jersey. I work in New York. I gotta come across them every day. I do not hate white people. I just don't trust most of them, that's all."

At the end of the night, Bernadette stayed over at his apartment, drinking cheap table wine with Vic and Rocky on the fire escape. Before they finally settled in for bed, she sat on the windowsill, contemplative. He watched her from the bathroom, where he brushed his teeth, knowing there was something on her mind. He finished up and sat on the bed in his boxers.

"You coming to bed or what?"

"I want to talk to you about something." He leaned back, giving her his full attention. "I have a decision to make soon. At the end of May, after finals, I can go back to Phoenix for the summer or I can stay here."

"Okay. What do you want to do?"

"What do you want me to do?"

"Nope. That is not my decision. I want you to do what you think is best for you."

"That's some bullshit. I want to hear from you, Rashid. What do you want from me? What do you want from this?"

"What? Where is this coming from?"

"I just . . . it would be nice to know sometime, like, what is it you want here? Like, is the way we are now just fine for you?"

He looked at her, focused on her eyes, the austerity of her cheekbones. It occurred to him that he'd had a similar conversation once with someone, someone he did not want to live without.

"I think where we are now is great," he said, a slight tremor in his voice. "Don't you?"

He was standing on the subway platform with Osman when his phone rang. It was Stacie's number, and he let it go straight to voice mail since the train was approaching. As he sat in the dentist's office waiting for the kid to be done with his appointment, he listened to his message. He heard an excited Stacie tell him she needed to see him right away. After dropping Osman off at his grandmother's place, he headed to the bookstore. There were about three customers hanging around, and he went straight to the register, where Stacie lunged at him and they embraced. He could not recall the last time he'd seen his cousin this enthused.

"I got the Micheaux Fellowship!" she burst out. He couldn't recall what she was referring to, and she explained it all as they took her lunch break and walked to Prospect Park. Back in the fall, her supervisor at her off-Broadway theatre in Manhattan had informed her of a fellowship that was designed to give writers of color the opportunity to work for film and television by pairing them with mentors in the entertainment industry. It was a long shot of course, but she had nothing to lose. She submitted thirty pages of her script on the life of Nina Simone and then waited. Two weeks ago, she had a phone interview with three of the people on the committee of the fellowship. She thought it went well, but she kept it to herself, not wanting to get too excited. This morning she got the email she had been waiting for: she had been accepted. The fellowship required her to move to Los Angeles for two years and work at the company's headquarters in Burbank. They would give her a monthly stipend, and she was almost guaranteed a job in the industry if she finished the program successfully. There was no way she could even consider rejecting the offer. His cousin had roughly four months to settle all of her affairs before moving across the country. The thought of her not being a train ride away was stifling to him. To his surprise, she shared his anguish.

"You can come with me," she said.

"What?"

"I don't know. It's crazy, but I was thinking about it. You're a great cook. You can cook anywhere. What's to stop you from coming with me? You can get a job at any of a thousand restaurants in LA. And I could use you there. I'm scared, Shid. This is a big move for me to make on my own."

He nodded, flattered, and a little taken aback. He had never been on a plane. He couldn't imagine a life outside New York City. He had no idea how to drive. They agreed that he would think about it. The first person he ran it by was Marlon.

"Shit, you couldn't pay me to live in no fucking Los Angeles. They got earthquakes, drought, all the women have these huge silicone titties. There's a phoniness out there, man. I'm telling you. They ain't like us. West Coast don't know shit about real life."

"How you know? You ain't ever even been, right?"

"Ain't you ever watched *Beverly Hills, 90210?*"

His mother was more positive.

"This could open up so many opportunities for you, son. You could get a job at one of them fancy restaurants out there. I've seen how some of them chefs roll. You could get you a job as a personal chef to Eddie Murphy!"

As much as he thought about it, he couldn't truly see it happening. He was a New Yorker through and through, a Brooklyn kid to the end. The very idea of living in a place with no subway system, with no ability to hail a taxi on the corner, with no winters, with no Yankees or Knicks, that was as appealing to him as what he imagined life to be on an Amish farm. It could never work. He wasn't built to live that way. And besides, he loved his job at Amalfi Sunset, he liked his living situation with Vic and Rocky, and he could never leave Osman now that he was the boy's godfather—the closest thing to a father the kid would probably ever know.

He shared these concerns with Stacie while they drank at the Amalfi bar one night shortly before closing. He was relieved to find her fully understanding and sympathetic. She presented him with another idea—go with her just for a week or so, help her get settled in.

At the end of August, they had a going-away party for Stacie at the house in Newark. Everyone they loved was there, even Marlon, who came with both of his girlfriends and his two sets of kids. The three of them toasted with gin and sodas on the back porch, while Stacie held his sleeping youngest child in her arms.

"Nigga, how you made this polygamous shit work out, I will never understand," Stacie commented. "Like you some Senegalese chief and shit."

"It's pretty simple," Marlon replied. "A man with as much charisma and appeal as myself, it's just too much for one woman to absorb on her own."

The next day, Rashid and Stacie were on a direct flight from LaGuardia to Los Angeles International Airport. She had found a nice one-bedroom apartment in the city of Glendale, and the two went shopping for furniture at various secondhand stores and consignment shops around town, hitting up a few garage sales as well. He was there a total of ten days, half of them alone with Stacie, and the second half they were joined by Bernadette who flew in from Phoenix. They all had a great time hitting up the beach almost every day, and he was comforted to learn that he was correct in his initial assessment—that as warm, aesthetically pleasing, and fun as Los Angeles was, it would never have been a good fit for him. The traffic alone was enough to give him headaches.

On their last night, they all dined out at a restaurant in Bel Air. After dinner they walked off the decadent meal with a stroll along Santa Monica beach. When they decided it was time to go, Stacie left them alone on the pier as she went to get the car. While staring out at the Pacific Ocean, he took Bernadette's hand in his.

"Hey, have you already made all your plans with the dorms and everything?"

"Uh, yes, hello, I head back to school in two weeks. Why?"

"I don't know, I was just thinking there is a studio apartment opening up in our building, and the landlord asked me if I'd be interested. I just thought maybe you would consider moving in with me."

"You jerk," she said, tossing his hand aside. "Now you bring this up to me, after I've already made all those plans."

They moved in together that October.

Nineteen

The next summer, Bernadette's family was coming to town for her graduation, and although he was anxious to finally meet her parents, who he had heard so many stories about, he wasn't truly excited about having to spend an entire week entertaining them. Bernadette had set up plans for them to spend practically every night of the week with her mom and dad, including Rashid's days off. These plans involved a Broadway show, three different museums, the Bronx Zoo, an opera, a Dance Theatre of Harlem performance, a Mets game, and maybe a Yankees game.

Bernadette's older sister, Felicity, a graduate student in psychology, had arrived a day earlier, and was staying on a borrowed futon in their studio apartment. She was friendly and unimposing, but she was afraid of the city. She had seen way too many movies and television shows and seemed to truly believe that a mugger or murderer could be lurking around every corner.

On Thursday night, her parents were arriving at John F. Kennedy Airport, and he went with Bernadette to pick them up while Felicity was in Manhattan visiting with a friend. In the baggage claim area, he sat with a cold soda in hand, waiting for Bernadette, who was upstairs trying to get details about their delayed arrival. A figure passed by, pulling a suitcase in one hand and a trumpet in another. The two of them recognized each other instantly. It was Rachel's brother. It always amazed him just how small New York could be at times.

Jerry McGill

They hugged and exchanged quick pleasantries. The brother had just returned from working on a recording session in Cleveland and was looking forward to spending some time at home before heading out to Amsterdam for a few weeks. Rashid shared that he was working at a new restaurant now and that he was actually the head chef. For some reason, he lied and said that he was planning on opening his own place next year in Queens, a Jamaican-themed venture. He had no idea why he said it, the words just spilled out of him. The brother congratulated him and said he would have to let him know when it opened.

"Where did you just come from?" the brother asked.

"Me? Oh, no, I am actually just here picking up someone. My girlfriend's parents are gonna be in town for a week."

"Girlfriend, huh? Good for you. It's funny, we were just talking about you last week. Rachel is staying with me for a bit, and she had gotten tickets for that revival of *The King and I* on Broadway, but she didn't want to go because she said it would remind her of you, so she gave me the tickets."

It hit him right away—the idea that she would seek to avoid being reminded of him.

"She's staying with you, huh? Is she okay?"

"Yeah, she's alright. It's temporary. She's hit on some hard times. Michael really turned the fire up on her on their divorce. She wound up just giving him full custody of the kids, which really was for the best. I honestly don't think Rachel was cut out to be a long-term mother. Hey, I'm sure she would love to hear from you sometime. You should stop by."

"Oh, I can't do that." He felt himself being pulled down under the waves. "I mean, it's not a good idea. I just barely got over Rachel, you know? It was hard on me. She was kind of the love of my life."

"Hey." The brother put a firm hand on his shoulder. "I get it, man. I fully get it. There's a reason why there are a billion songs about love, ya know? A damned good reason. If you're ever in the area, I still have

178

a once-a-month gig at the Honey Pot. Bernice is not with us anymore, but I got this new chick from Nigeria, just kills it nightly. Would be great to see you."

When they hugged farewell, he could smell the marijuana on the brother's clothes, and it took him to a place he had thought he'd put behind him. Bernadette eventually showed up with her exhausted parents, and they all talked on the drive to their Manhattan hotel. They seemed to be just as nice as Rashid imagined they would be, but he was barely able to stay in the present with them. He couldn't shake the idea that Rachel was somewhere out there, nearby. Within reach.

After attending Bernadette's graduation ceremony, they went into Manhattan, where they proceeded to take a series of photos in Central Park. After an early dinner at Tavern on the Green, they split up and called it a night. Felicity and the younger sister, Melanie, were both staying with Rashid and Bernadette now, and on the drive home, he listened as the sisters sang pop songs at the top of their lungs to the radio. He found their spontaneity and fervor engaging, but he could not help but feel a gaping distance from them. That night, he stayed upstairs with Vic and Rocky, giving the sisters some space to catch up and bond.

The next day Bernadette's entire crew was heading out to the Jersey Shore and then on to Coney Island. He was supposed to join them, but he had already made up his mind that he couldn't do it. He had a pressing matter to attend to, and so he lied to her and told her that he had been called into work unexpectedly. Once she was gone, he showered, shaved, and rushed out of the apartment. He caught a taxi and went straight to the block where the brother lived. There was a diner across the street from the brother's apartment, and he sat in that diner by a window that gave him an ideal view of the entrance to the brother's building.

He ordered coffee. Then about a half hour later, he ordered a second cup. Then scrambled eggs. The waitress, a middle-aged woman with a European accent, didn't seem to care how long he stayed. The place was only half-full, and she continued refilling his coffee cup. All the while, he kept his eyes on the entrance. He wondered if it was crazy to be spying on them like this, and he questioned what he hoped to get out of it all. He knew he didn't want to talk to Rachel—had no intention of engaging her—but if he could just see her for himself. To just see her—there could be something in the act. Something, he didn't know how to view it, healing?

At about the two-and-a-half-hour mark, he got his wish. She walked out of the building wearing sunglasses, a long, flowing, tie-dye skirt, and a black Rolling Stones T-shirt. She had gained some weight, that was easy enough to gather. Her hips filled the skirt in a more voluptuous way than she ever had in the past, and her face seemed richer, more layered. Her hair was pulled back in a tight ponytail, but a few strands had broken loose and dangled down across her left cheek. She was standing there outside the building, just leaning against the wall. The sun was strong and seemed to be pinning her to the wall, but she appeared not to notice it. A man walked by and said something to her, and she ignored him. All of a sudden he wanted to rise. Instead, he just watched her.

She pulled something out of her purse, it was a cell phone, and she checked it. She started pushing buttons. She was texting someone. The waitress startled him by asking him if he was ready for the check, and he held out his cup for one more refill. When she was done and gone, he turned his attention back across the street. His anxiety turned to grief as he watched a taxi pull up, watched her get in, and watched it disappear down the street.

"I never want you to hate me," she had once said to him. There was no chance that could ever happen, he had told her then. He could confirm it now. He paid his bill and headed for the subway.

That night Bernadette came home with her sisters, and they all went out to the bar across the street. They sat across from each other in a booth, he and Bernadette on one side, the sisters on the other.

Bernadette was rubbing his thigh, and every now and then, she turned to him and kissed his cheek. He was a lucky man and he knew it. Just hours ago he had felt guilty about going to see Rachel, about camping outside the brother's house and essentially stalking his ex-lover. The part that made him feel the worst was that he had lied to Bernadette earlier. Had looked her in the face and created an absolute fiction. But he remembered something Stacie had told him not long ago: "The truth, it can be overrated . . . Sometimes we're just better off not knowing things."

Somewhere between the subway station and their apartment, he had realized something: it was all necessary. If he and Bernadette were to ever have a true future, then that afternoon had to happen. It all made sense to him. Bumping into the brother could not have been a coincidence.

"There are no coincidences," Marlon had once said when they were in junior high school.

As the sisters went on and on about some night when they were in high school and had all gotten drunk after a football game, he sat there and took in Bernadette's features. He loved her, there was no doubting it. He still loved Rachel too, there was no doubting that either. And he was concluding that it was okay. Love did not need to be all or nothing; it was not a zero-sum game. Love was a lot like one of those gorgeous symphonies Rachel had introduced him to. There were gradations and fluctuations, crescendos, crests, fortissimo, and eventually, at some point, the inevitable diminuendo. No movement lasted forever, but the really special ones reverberated through time and rested in your bloodstream as long as you breathed. Because he loved Rachel, his love for Bernadette could be even richer. This was the gig.

Love was like a newborn child—beautiful, fragile, at risk. And somewhere along the way, at some point on the journey, it would disappoint you. Make you question why you ever allowed it in. It was never going to be satisfactory, full and whole. It would be pieces of memories, songs, bits of discussions, images, oh so many images, all strung together like a beaded necklace.

He felt hope. It was just the beginning of the summer.

Shiny bodies pressed together that afternoon in the kitchen, colliding and bouncing off one another like hopped-up dancers in a popular nightclub. He had already sweated fully through one white shirt and went quickly to the back office to change into a second one. It was on days like these that he wished he had never quit smoking. It was also on days like these that he briefly wished he had stayed a waiter. The air was much cooler out on the floor of Amalfi Sunset. But he shook his head and laughed that thought away.

While in the back office, he checked his email quickly on Mario's computer. He updated the day's menu and placed several orders for food supplies. It was crazy to him just how many emails one could receive in a twenty-four-hour period. There was news about changes to this week's shipment of shrimp, there was one from his mother forwarding a newspaper article on the hottest restaurants in Brooklyn (of which Amalfi Sunset was one), and there was an email from Bernadette that featured tourist attractions in Milan. The two of them were heading there in October as part of a work-related trip Mario had arranged. His passport had just arrived in the mail that week.

Rashid felt his phone buzz in his pocket, and he went to check it. It was from the Comforti's host desk. He assumed it was Lucia checking in to see if their lunch date for next week was still on. He answered and heard the dulcet voice of the new German hostess, Sasha. She let him know that an "old lady" had called there looking for him. She had asked Sasha to forward her phone number to him and ask him to call her right away at his earliest convenience. He scurried for a pen and paper to write Muriel's number down. He had never expected to hear from Muriel again.

He looked at the clock on the computer. It would be an hour until the dinner rush kicked in, so he had time. He dialed her number.

"Hello, Muriel?"

She sounded worn out, overly tired, which was to be expected. There was a slur in her tone, which strained communication some. She told him how she'd had a difficult time locating him. That his old phone number no longer worked. He told her he thought of her often. She asked him if he would come see her, she had some important information to share. Rashid offered to meet the next week. Muriel preferred if he came sooner. She had sad news—Rachel had died a few days ago. The words "Rachel died" lodged in his chest and caused lumps the size of cherry pits to seize his throat. He asked her if he could come over right away. She said she'd be waiting for him.

The lobby was exactly the same, not one change that he could notice. Even the friendly Black doorman was still there, like a minor character in a dated television comedy: "Welcome back, sir. Long time no see!"

Her apartment was also the same, but now she had a full-time care attendant, a portly Haitian woman with youthful skin who smiled warmly as she led him to her. Muriel was seated on the couch watching television intently. As he approached her, he realized she was watching some kind of documentary with footage of the planes hitting the Twin Towers. The familiar, gruesome scene gave him an uneasy feeling. Muriel had put on some weight, and she leaned heavily on her right side, where her arm sat folded under her like a fleshy stool. She smelled of caked-up flesh and baby oil. Time had not been as kind to her as it could have. When she noticed him, she fished desperately around her with her one arm flailing.

"*Marcia, where is my remote control? Shut this shit off now!*"

Once the attendant had brought him a cup of chamomile tea with a lemon wedge, he settled in. There was something unnerving and awful about the room. One lamp lit them poorly; most of the light

183

emanated from the TV screen, which had been paused on the moment right before the second plane struck. He deliberately put his back to it and watched her. She spoke in a slow and practiced pace, as if full sentences were an effort. He listened carefully, hanging on every word. When he brought his cup to his lips, his hand shook a little. She told him everything.

Rachel had gone back to the home and the husband. She had hoped that perhaps the third time would be the charm, but nothing had changed. She had pretty much hated the husband but vowed to keep up the charade until the youngest had at least started high school. She got a job editing a classical music magazine, but still had her hopes set on a university position. She interviewed as often as she could, and the rejection slowly ate away at her. Eventually she left the husband and took up various house-sitting jobs all around the country.

A groundskeeper had found her body in the early morning hours outside her hotel in Atlanta. The day before, she had interviewed with Georgia State University. She had told her mother it "seemed promising." Sometime after three a.m. she jumped from the balcony of her sixteenth-floor hotel room. She had not left a note, but she had called the husband and left him a voice mail right around that time. She told him to always remind the kids that she had loved them and to do so even more around the holidays. She had been wearing the same black-and-red suit from her interview.

On the subway ride to Muriel's apartment, he had wondered—how did the old lady know to call him? How did she know he would care? She anticipated his question. When the son found out about his sister's death, he had told Muriel that she should call him. The son had told her everything about them—about the weekends at his apartment, about the date nights at his club. The son had told her that he genuinely believed they were in love.

He apologized to her, apologized for keeping it a secret. He started to cry.

"Don't do that. Don't you apologize for anything. I'm glad you loved her. I'm glad somebody loved her. She deserved it. God knows I could never do a good job of it. I was too bitter."

Rashid had one question for her, something he had always wanted to know. He told her about the picture he had taken from her home that day. He had forgotten to ask Rachel about it, but he had always wanted to know—what was she doing in that picture? What was its origin? Muriel apologized. She couldn't remember.

He left her. As the attendant opened the door for him, he turned to her.

"How long has she been watching that?"

"Longer than I care to remember," she replied.

On the subway ride home, he became overwhelmed with sadness at the thought of Rachel all alone in that hotel room. How profoundly without support she must have felt. Was there really no one in her life she could have turned to? What does it take to walk out on a balcony and look down and see the answer to your suffering far below on the cold, hard pavement? He wondered if, when she'd looked up at the moon in that moment, she'd had any idea just how iridescent its shadow had made her skin look their first night together and every night together after that. Should he have told her that more often? He remembered how she'd looked early in the summer when he'd watched her from the diner across the street. What if he had just gone over and talked to her then? Could he have changed her fate? Was it even possible to change one's fate? After all, your fate is your fate, isn't it? He buried his wet face in his hands and wept at questions that could never be answered. For promise unfulfilled. There were so many ways the world could kill you.

He saw the brother again. He decided to go to the jazz club one last time to give himself closure. The brother joined him at the bar after the first set ended. They shook hands like awkward lovers on a blind date. He asked the brother about the picture. The brother said he couldn't remember all the details, but he was almost certain it was from a day camp they once attended in the summer on a horse farm. Rachel had always hated it. She hated the smell of horses. She feared their angry snorts. The brother walked him out and asked him to stay in touch. Rashid lied and said he would try. He could see that the brother's eyes were immersed in tears. He wanted to reach out to him, but he didn't know that language with the brother.

"I just don't understand how this could happen to someone twice. Back when I was in college, I once loved a girl. She took her life too. Same fucking thing . . ."

He knew the story. He recalled how Rachel had said the girl "did an Anna Karenina."

"I mean, with all that is so beautiful in this world, why does someone with so much choose that? I mean, look at us—are we not fortunate? Look at that guy carrying those flowers? Is he not fortunate?" The brother was pointing to a man in a suit carrying a bouquet of roses. "Look at that woman with her laundry? Is she not fortunate?" The brother was pointing to a gorgeous woman in leather pants walking down the street with a bag full of laundry in her hands. "I mean, doesn't all of this beat the alternative?"

"I don't know. Maybe that's easy for you and me to say. I don't have an answer."

He went to visit his mother. He knew he wouldn't share his anguish with her; besides the fact that she never knew about Rachel, he also didn't want to burden her. He just wanted to be near her.

"How's my daughter-in-law?" she teased.

"She's good, Ma. The Jesuits didn't ruin her."

"She gonna stay here with us or what?"

He had informed her recently that Bernadette had a choice to make: do her graduate work here in the city, or do so back in her home state where it would be cheaper.

"She will do whatever is best for her, Ma."

"I'm sure she wouldn't mind hearing that you would like her to stay."

He thought about this statement. He thought about what it meant when you told someone you wanted them in your life. He thought about the many things left unsaid with Rachel. She had wanted to give him a letter. His throat clenched and his voice cracked.

"People are gonna do what they're gonna do. You need to accept that, Ma."

He sat with Marlon in a park, and they watched his two kids playing on the swing. Seeing all the kids in the park made him reflect on Rachel's children. He wondered again how someone could do such a thing knowing the effect it could have on their children. He remembered the angry son. He shared with Marlon that he imagined her kids would be scarred eternally, irreparably.

"That's very likely so," Marlon responded. "But that's the thing about pain, man. It can be all-consuming, clouds everything, all judgment."

"I just don't understand why she didn't reach out to somebody. Anybody."

"Trust me, as someone who has been there—sometimes there is nobody."

"Nigga, when were you there? You never told me about it."

"We don't always say everything that we feel, now do we? Especially us men, we ain't supposed to talk about that shit. Don't you worry, I was there and I came through it. But don't underestimate it. It's hard shit. It's why I can't judge someone who couldn't get through it. She's in good company."

Rashid found he could barely get out of bed. He called in sick three days in a row. He was fortunate in that Bernadette was out of town visiting an ailing uncle, and would be there a few more days. The last thing he needed was to explain everything to her. Why he wasn't eating, wasn't showering, wasn't shaving. Why the mattress was like a black hole, devouring him, holding him down. He listened to classical music a lot, thought about the old lady sitting there in her apartment with her aide. He realized he could not let himself become that. He could not allow life to do that to him. He started receiving texts from Stacie:

> Just got my tenth rejection on the Katrina pilot.

> Hardest shit I've ever written and people out here don't give two fucks.

> Systems fail Black and brown people all the time.

> Let's move to Mombasa, run a bed-and-breakfast. I'll start my romance novel about Black vampires living on a farm in Utah.

She had worked diligently on a television pilot about a Black family living in the aftermath of Hurricane Katrina, a topic that bordered on obsession with her. She had even gone to New Orleans to conduct personal interviews on two occasions. She was hoping to do a documentary on it someday. He texted her back:

> I'm afraid of dengue fever. Please send me a postcard when you get there.

She texted back:

> You are an idiot.

He smiled, grateful for the reprieve from thinking about Muriel at home sitting on the couch watching a plane crash into a building over and over. He could imagine her strong opinion on something like Hurricane Katrina: "Hundreds of people sat in their living rooms watching the water rise above their heads. And they were all asking—where is God?"

Eventually he got out of bed, showered, and put fresh clothes on. The world had to go on, this much he knew. When he got to work that afternoon, Mario remarked dryly, "Oh look, Sleeping Beauty has emerged from her slumber." Without responding, Rashid went to the office, checked his emails, and proceeded to put in his first full day in nearly a week.

He went to Sonia's house to pick up Osman. The kid would be starting at a new school shortly, and Sonia had given them $500, a gift from the Comfortis, with which to go clothes shopping. They walked along the Grand Concourse, darting in and out of various stores. They decided to take a break at a local ice cream shop. Over caramel-fudge sundaes, they talked.

"Say, I wanna ask you about something. Do you know what depression is?"

"Yeah, it's like when you're sad, right?"

"Yeah, yeah, it is."

"My mother says she and my uncle Chucho get depression sometimes. I think Uncle Chucho takes medicine for it."

"Do you ever get sad?"

He scanned the kid's face and could tell that he was going down an unnecessary road; the kid didn't have a care in the world, and he envied him.

"Nah, I'm a pretty happy guy."

"Of course you are. You and your ice-cream stained shirt." They laughed together as he dipped his napkin in a cup of water and blotted at a newly formed chocolate stain on the kid's white shirt. "You know that if you ever did feel sad, you could talk to me about it, right?"

"Yeah."

"Don't just 'Yeah' me."

"Yeah, man, what you want?"

"I want to hear you say it—'If I'm ever sad, I'll talk to my *papi* Rashid about it.'"

The kid responded in a mocking tone. "If I'm ever sad, I'll talk to my *papi* Rashid about it."

"Say that shit like you mean it, okay?"

Again, mocking him. "Say that shit like you mean it, okay?"

He dotted the kid's nose with ice cream from his spoon, and the two of them laughed. He knew that he would love the kid forever, a sensation that brought him much joy, but also scared him a little.

One afternoon, on the way into the city to pick up ingredients, he went to count the rats at the Nostrand Avenue station, and to his complete awe, he did not spot one, which never seemed possible to him. He couldn't believe his eyes, and he looked up and down the rails several times before the train came. Later, as he sat on a bench in the park across the street from Amalfi Sunset during his break, he texted the only person in the world he knew would care.

NO RATS TODAY DURING COUNT THE RATS! FIRST
TIME EVER! BET THE LOTTERY!
GET OUT!

THAT CAN'T BE! YOU ARE LOSING YOUR EYESIGHT!
Seriously, that is most likely a sign of the apocalypse.

Are you free to talk for a few?

His phone rang thirty seconds later. Hearing her voice would always have a soothing effect on him.

"What's happening, hot stuff?"

"Oh, you know. Another day in the kitchen."

"Chef it up, Black man. Hey, guess what? My schedule has shifted some. It's looking like I'll be able to join you and Bernie for a week in Milan. I'm gonna start a new show in the fall, a spin-off of *Twin City Sisters*. It's basically a silly soap opera about all these Black nurses and doctors in Minneapolis, but it's gonna make me very comfortable financially."

They talked for a half hour about the best ways to travel through Europe, caught up on life, their jobs. He was due back in the kitchen soon, but he couldn't bring himself to get off the phone with her just yet.

"Hey, can I ask you a question?"

"Sure you can, but be quick. I've got yoga in Venice Beach in an hour. I'm turning into that person who is addicted to yoga on the beach."

"Have you ever known anyone who committed suicide?"

"Hmm, other than my father? Thankfully, no. There was a girl at the bookstore, Tamika, she was, like, a Barnard student or something, she talked about it from time to time, made a lot of us uncomfortable. She was struggling with grades and adapting to city life and blah blah. She wrote a lot of dark poetry. Why do you ask?"

"I just found out an old close friend of mine committed suicide, and it's been hard, very hard to accept."

"Oh, I'm sorry, boo. That's gotta be tough. We have all these ideas about suicide—that it's selfish, that it's a choice. It's funny you bring it up, because I've been researching this lately for a project I'm working on—and the truth is that a lot of times, a person who chooses to do that is so far gone, they really, truly believe the world and everyone in their lives would be better off without them."

"Which is hard for me to fathom. I mean, she had two kids. How are they ever gonna overcome that?"

"They'll manage. It will take time, but they'll manage. Or they won't. At the end of the day, it will be one or the other. We all basically have two choices—move forward or move back. I'm sorry if that sounds cold."

"It sounds realistic. I should let you go."

"Yeah, traffic is a bitch out here. Hey, I'm sorry about your friend. But remember, this existence is not for everybody. I've been thinking about Icarus a lot lately. I'm halfway through writing a play that's kind of a modern feminist take on it."

"Icarus?"

"Yeah, you know—had wings made of wax, flew too close to the sun, fell to the earth."

"Oh yeah, that guy."

"Yeah, well you know the general consensus is that Icarus was foolish and prideful, that a blatant disregard for the rules caused him to disobey his father and fly too close to the sun. But I like to argue that we've looked at it in the wrong light. That in actuality, Icarus became enchanted by the sun, and as he flew towards it, the very idea of it, the unparalleled magnificence of the sun, was so stunningly precious that he couldn't stop himself. He knew in his heart of hearts that he was leaving a hideous place behind him and edging ever closer to one of untold beauty. And the thing is, once you decide, once you put yourself on that straight and narrow path towards the sun, you can't have second thoughts. There is no turning back. Once you feel that warmth on your face, it's already too late for you."

There was a long silence between them, as the words found their way across the thousands of miles that separated them and landed softly, like butterflies, on his chest.

"Anyway, that's all I got, cuz."

When he hung up and put his phone away, he sat on the bench a long time. He was at least fifteen minutes overdue on his break, and people were probably waiting for him to get orders in. None of it mattered. Many thoughts went through his mind. He saw a clear image of Rachel on a balcony in the night, looking up at the moon and maybe seeing the sun. He reached for a pack of cigarettes in his shirt pocket and remembered that he had quit smoking. He would need something to replace that habit. He made a mental note to pick up a new flute.

Acknowledgments

So many wonderful people were a part of this book coming to life. I have unwavering affection and gratitude to my agent, Priya Doraswamy, who saw something in me few others in this industry could. To my editors Laura Van der Veer and Angie Chatman, thank you for finding value in my story and choosing and shaping my words. To my favorite and most loving feedback loop—Zora and Ariana—thanks for adding flesh to the bones. I wouldn't be a published writer today were it not for the support of allies Lorrie Moore and Hana Mundhe.

Eternal thanks to Willie Reale, Carol Ochs, Kirsten Aspengren, Mark Hansen, Lidia Yuknavitch, Shalom Auslander, Nora Spiegel, Miriam Kley, Terrance Hayes, and the Vermont Studio Center.

About the Author

Jerry McGill is a writer and artist. He is the author of a memoir, *Dear Marcus: A Letter to the Man Who Shot Me*. After receiving a BA in English literature from Fordham University in the Bronx and a master's degree in education from Pacific University in Oregon, Jerry went on to teach high school and travel the world mentoring disabled children. He lives in Portland, Oregon.